Creole Fire

Tayannah Lee McQuillar

This book is dedicated to P.B. Randolph, Angelo Solimon, Joseph Bologne, Jarena Lee, Percy Julian, John Michell, Benjamin Bradley, Mother Leafy Anderson, Martin Delany, Pauline Hopkins and countless other unnamed Black intellectuals, geniuses and mystics (past and present) that have been humiliated, ignored, discredited, diminished, robbed or purposely forgotten.

Paschal Beverly Randolph

ACKNOWLEDGMENTS

I wish to express my gratitude to John Patrick Deveny for his wonderful biography, Paschal Beverly Randolph: A Nineteenth Century Black American Spiritualist, Rosicrucian and Sex Magician.

I sincerely thank the following writers/scholars for their positive and thought provoking contributions to the study of African diasporic religious/spiritual traditions and/or Creole culture. The Augustine/Comeaux family (frenchcreoles.com), Yvonne Chireau (author of *Black Magic*), Katrina Hazzard-Donald (author of *Mojo Workin'*), Stephen Finley, Margarita Guillory and Hugh Page Sr. (editors of *Esotericism in African American Religious Experience*), Wonda L. Fontenot (author of *Secret Doctors*), Creole historian Barbara Trevigne and Mama Zogbe (mamiwata.com). Your hard work and dedication is greatly appreciated.

PART ONE

"If greatness consists partly in doing and producing much with means which, in the hands of the others, would have been insufficient, then Randolph possesses that constituent of greatness. If greatness means power and ingeniousness to concentrate the gifts and talents of many on one point, to inspire others with sympathy and enthusiasm for the same end, and to make them gladly contribute toward it, then he was great. If it is great to see from the earliest manhood the main end of one's individual life, steadily pursuing it to the very end with the highest gifts of nature, then he was great. If greatness means to soar high in the one selected sphere; to be trivial or puerile in none—on the contrary, to retain a vivid sympathy with all that is noble, beautiful, true and just, then he was great. If it is a characteristic of greatness to be original and strike out on new paths; indeed, even to prophetic anticipations, then he was great. If greatness requires marked individuality, which yet takes up all the main threads that give distinctness to the times we live in, then he was great. If greatness means an inventive and interleaguing imagination that gathers what is scattered, and, grandly simplifies and unites the details, and rears a temple, then he was great, for his mind and Soul possessed greatness. Truly great men are not jealous and are void of envy. They are full of inspiring ambition, but free from a desire to keep competitors down. Randolph showed no envy, or anything else that destroys true greatness."

-Contemporary of P.B. Randolph

CHAPTER ONE

"When it is asserted that there is no mysterious means whereby ends both good and ill can be wrought at any distance; that the so called "spells", "charms" and "projects" are mere notions, having no firmer foundation than superstition or empty air alone; -- then I flatly deny all such assertions, and affirm that the conclusions arrived at are so reached by persons wholly ignorant of the invisible world about us, and of the inner powers of the human mind."

– P.B. RANDOLPH

June 1864

1

The quadroon orphan that conjured and cured

Travelled the world seeking a womb in which to mature

In tailored frock and elaborate cravat, he arrived quite pretty

With skin of *café au lait et cheveux ondules* he'd be welcome in the crescent city

But there was no place on earth without the stench of his mother's death

Nor any strong hand to replace the first man to teach a boy discipline and depth

So off to London! Off to Paris! On a Persian rug he shall fly!

To escape the gaping wound and repair it too, this the orphan did not deny

Despite all the woes, there is much he knows from being self-taught.

A supreme grand master teacher he is and a receptacle of the most brilliant gnosis,

But the African blood in his veins prevented the world from proclaiming his apotheosis.

He thought, "wouldn't it be wonderful if my dark eyes came from a batik clad Malay?

Isn't it true I would get my due if I could wash the Negro away?

The world said no, you're still a bro and for that you'll always lack

No intellectual peaks, it's all the Greeks! Greatness does not come in Black.

2

Paschal Beverly Randolph is what the birth certificate said

But what is that but another trap for the mentally dead?

The mirror may lie about your past but it always reflects the soul

Only in the hands of an expert scryer like "the Rosicrucian" can the real truth be told

He has many tricks up his sleeves, in powdered leaves and in his pants

The doctor's dick is excelcior because of the spirit within it, should you be worthy of a dance

Brothers of electricity, ether and the eternal waters I implore you to pleasure your sisters!

Lessons to waste not your elixir and test the yoni frowns the faces of lesser misters.

They are the unwashed, that's why they scoff so of them attention do not pay

For all they seek is frolic, sleep and meat not the bliss of agape

He saw Esau inside himself and other men as he sailed the seven seas

The reality did not please him, nor did the reasons so farewell life of ease!

Now what should you do? Seek the voudeax! He said as he packed pestle and mortar

With the *gens de couleur libres* and other believers, I'll live in the French Quarter.

3

He pats the soot off his clothes and covers his nose as he disembarks the train

Those deep set eyes scan the scenery far and wide, this student of Cagliostro and Saint Germain

Two dark haired beauties thought 'he's a cutie' before they demurely diverted their eyes

Then one of them speaks, he wanted to shriek! Until he got a surprise

She was a mess in her satin dress and cheap floral brooch

She smiled and extended a torn gloved hand ---perhaps before the war her charms were beyond reproach

Paschal slightly tipped his hat and shook one lacy finger for this was certainly no lady

Her teeth were rotten and a glaring man in the distance told him this woman was shady

Easing passed the prostitute he stepped into a waiting carriage

"Quickly to the Vieux Carré!" he called before his reputation was irreparably damaged

As he rolled along towards the city he heard pleas for bread and many sorrowful songs

The Civil War brought poverty, pain and death to all, be they right or wrong

As quick as a flash a black cat scurried by and met its death under a shoddy wheel

Two starving children in rags saw no tragedy but instead a much needed meal.

4

The black boots of the Union army stomped heavy upon extricated confederate hearts

Paschal nodded at the recently emancipated men proudly discussing the building of ramparts

To *General Phelps! To Phelps! A drunk Negro cheered as he staggered passed,

The driver quipped "You see dis shit?" as if he had to ask

Doctor Randolph straightened his coat, how dare this man use such a familiar tone?

I am hierarch of the Ansaireh! Don't make me hit you with my philosophers stone!

"Where you won go Suh?" inquired the ignorant peasant. "Who you tryna meet?"

"I'm here to visit a woman I heard about that lives on St. Ann's street."

The peasant laughed and scratched his ass "I already know, cuz you look like the type dat go tuh see LaVeau."

Doctor Randolph sniffed and let out a hiss that the man thought he had him figured out

"Don't fret yoself none but let me tell ya wut she's all about."

"Fancy man be careful or you'll get a root put on ya by that witch

Go see Doctor John instead, don't be trussin that stuck up bitch!

*John Wolcott Phelps (1813 – 1885), was a general in the Union Army and an abolitionist.

5

The old adobe cottage said the voud had no money yet everyone knew her name

So it was with famous Sufis dwelling in simple tents, it was all the same

A host of colored children played games and ran

As an Octoroon closely eyed the mole on the back of his hand

"Come with me, since you're too good to wait," she winked,

Paschal smirked at the handsome woman "Oh, is that what you think?"

Herbs hung over the door and the house smelled like moss

In front of a closed door with chalk drawings she made the sign of the cross

You came to see my mother but I'm just as good, sit down and put your hat over there

My name is Marie-Philomene and now *I* run *Congo Square!

Her power, her spirit and two renegade curls inspired a raging lust

'The lamp of Eulis is lit' whispered a phantom guide, of this fact you must certainly trust

He thought, "If I told Philomene what my third eye hath seen, would she be vexed or pleased?

The guide touched the spine to erect the snake, "Canst thou minister to a mind diseased?"

*Congo Square was a space where Blacks could express themselves culturally.

6

Philomene felt the cobra rise high above her head and closed her eyes to fate

Mère told her Le Sirene would send a man soon and the temptation would be great

A weakness she had for colored men with dark eyes and old souls.

With him, she could be so much more than she was today

Adieu Monsieur Legendre, laissez les bons temps rouler!

She awoke from her fantasy, it was plump and ripe, as he stared from across the table

Paschal sent another message from his mind, "Bite it Philomene, You know of what I'm able."

How would he part his lips as she moved her hips if she let him in?

She couldn't believe her thoughts, that's not how she was taught, "He must be a sex magician!"

7

The gardenias then screamed to the magus, "She's into you but onto you, so don't insult her by playing dumb,"

"Fore if you do, then the game is through and she will never give you some."

"Pardon me Ma'am, I must tell you the sky just opened up for me,"

"Light from the seventh heaven shone upon your face, have you heard of it? Hold not to my nose an imposter fluer de lis."

Philomene smirked and reached for a small pouch of satin amidst a dish of stones

Without removing her eyes from the tea sipping Samedi, she poured out the chicken bones

The wish and breast fell on the left, confirming the start of something new

"Toss that shell to your right so I can read the sign and then I must say goodbye to you."

"Dr. Randolph, Paschal is the name but don't say it to yourself too much,"

"It will be harder to pretend that you're not in love with me and then you'll never escape my clutch."

Philomene rubbed her thumb against her forefinger three times before she touched his chin,

"The act is cute city boy but we both know I'm the one that reeled *you* in!"

"What else do you see with the mutilated corpse of an unfortunate foul?"

She scooped the bones up once more and when they fell, her face formed an ugly scowl

"I hear a shot, loud screams and your tears upon the window of a funeral train,"

"A powerful friend will soon meet his end and you will be in great pain."

8

That night, Paschal watched the spectacle of thunder from the balcony of the hotel

Why had he come to this place of iron lace to behold visions of hell?

Obviously the Spanish seeded their sorrowful songs in Louisiana's womb

Macabre and passionate, severe and beautiful were those bones, as white as those sun bleached tombs

Randolph got drenched in the rain and tilted his face toward the shining moon

"I will follow you anywhere my love, I beg you to release me soon."

The shining crescent turned to her favorite star and asked, "Are you insane?"

"Look not upon my face anymore that way or I will remove you from this plane!"

Randolph sighed and went inside after his woman put him in his place again

She was the only one he was ever loyal to because she never forced a when

Why did his new fascination not want to participate in the most sacred rite?

LaVeau petite had captured the only world in which he dwelled, why did she not want to spend the night?

Paschal removed his clothes, blew out the candles and lay nude upon the bed

Philomene appeared in a gown of sheer ivory which let him know the reason --

The fascination was already wed.

9

The great priestess eyeballed her daughter as she stirred a pot of red beans and rice

"That man is all over you and it ain't even been fourteen days, just make sure you're willing to pay the price."

"I'm not leaving Emile for him mama, of that you can be sure,

He comes by for a drink or two now and then but I told him I'm not his cure."

"Yes, you told me that before cherie but I'm begging you to stay away,"

"You're almost thirty years old, no one else will want a woman going gray!"

Philomene swung her hair over the other shoulder and folded her arms

"Everyone knows I'm hotter than a banana foster and Randolph would marry me for my charms."

Madame LaVeau put down her wooden spoon and embraced her daughter

"Married or not that's not the kind of man that can stay. Don't you see his soul belongs to the water?"

Philomene kissed her mother's cheek, "Don't worry!" and she looked deep into her eyes

"I have a gris gris and twenty spirits that help me to act as my keepers and spies."

Madame LaVeau shook her head and wagged a finger in Philomene's face

"Believe it or not, there is nothing in heaven or on Earth that will keep that man in place."

July 1864

10

"New Orleans is hot because she exhales," thought Paschal as he walked to Rue St Ann

The sun told him it would be a special day but exactly what, he had no idea of the plan

As he turned the corner lined with bougainvillea, he spotted a man laughing with Philomene

He was the color of Mississippi mud but judging from his clothes and the posture he posed, he was clearly a man of means

Randolph stroked his beard and calmed his fears, it might not be what it seemed

The man straightened his coat as the beige man approached and extended his hand in a display quite haughty and lavish,

"This is Lieutenant James Hollings, he's a regular client of mine. He lives in Plaquemines Parish."

The three went inside the house and assembled themselves around

"Philomene told me all about you. Did you know your name is all over town?"

"I was completely unaware as I have only lectured a few times and sold tonic,"

"For me to achieve such notoriety for what to me is commonplace, would be quite ironic."

Hollings laughed and nodded his head, "I would be happy to hear an intelligent man speak."

"Thank you kind sir, I am happy to report that the next event will be held next week."

Hollings clapped his hands "How splendid! May I ask what the subject of your speech will be?"

"I am defending the abolitionist cause and I will not stop until there is no more slavery."

11

Philomene's eyes were suddenly filled with dread and her nerves appeared frayed

"Now let's not get into all that right now. Ya'll want some lemonade?"

Hollings waved his hand dismissively with his eyes flashing with rage

"It's people like you that will ruin our children's future in the coming age!"

Paschal looked quizzically at Philomene as Hollings' cusses came faster and faster,

It took a minute before he understood the reason for the Black man's anger, he was a prosperous slave master!

"Yeah I own Clavijo plantation and my sister owns niggers too,"

"She's in Charleston also trying desperately to keep what's hers because of people like you!"

Paschal blinked back painful tears as Hollings justified being a confederate

He too agreed that Negroes had no past but this man was a complete degenerate!

"Philomene, thank you for your offer but I think it's time to take my leave,

"If I listen to any more of this man's words, I fear my heart will forever grieve."

Hollings stood up at the same time as the doctor and blocked the door

"Yankees rob you of everything then they say they don't want to hear anymore!"

12

Paschal sat back down and crossed his legs because he understood the desire to be heard

21

Though Hollings position sickened him, he would listen without saying a word

Philomene cleared her throat and sat down at her Hoodoo table

"If things get too hot then take it outside, I want the spirit of this house to be stable."

Hollings took a deep breath, looked towards the sky and returned to his seat

"I apologize thoroughly for the sparks but on this point, I shall never retreat."

Doctor Randolph said "I accept your apology but slave owners I cannot respect,"

"The suffering caused by that institution is unfathomable, I'm sorry sir but I must object."

"So to you, from your point of view my ways are less than a beast,"

"But may I ask if it's true that you travel to and fro seeking the light of the East?"

Paschal cleared his throat and replied "I am a seeker of wisdom and knowledge wherever it may reside,"

"Germany, Scotland, France but I admit Egypt, Arabia and Turkey are my pride."

Hollings leaned back, crossed his legs and his lips curled into a smirk

"Look at you, you hypocrite! Who is a bigger slave master since time began than the Egyptians, Arabs and Turks?"

13

Philomene stared at the blue veins running through her palms as her friends tore each other apart,

She didn't understand why Paschal cared so much about Negroes since he was born free from the start

All three were lucky the good lord shared his blessings by making them all part white

What will happen to their special place in the world if the Union wins the fight?

They'll be lumped together with the niggers that used to swing from trees --- and treated even more mean

Philomene let out an internal scream, "That's not fair! Look at my hair and my eyes are almost green!"

She was proud when James became a lieutenant of the native guard

If the rich creoles in the city had no money to spend on ju-ju, times would get real hard

But she can't forget no matter how she looks, her grandmother's flesh was split by the lash,"

It's sad n true but what you gonna do? Breed out the problem then we'll have some cash!

Why couldn't Randolph see Hollings like she did as a symbol of Black power?

He's very rich and never dug a single ditch --these abolitionists are proverbially dour!

It would be nice but there ain't no place on God's green Earth where equality is true

So lose that dream in a fat ole cloud and get to doing what you gotta do.

14

"I've heard your thesis Hollings and you've heard mine so let's just leave it at that,"

"Surely we have something in common that is worthy of a chat."

Hollings shook his head and smiled, "You're sure good with people you know,"

"All I can see is we're both colored and free visiting la maison de Laveau."

Philomene laughed and slapped her knee

"There's more for you to twine on then that, believe you me."

Paschal and Hollings looked at each other before the doctor said "Well, why don't you tell us?"

"You both lost a mama and want another man's woman cuz ya'll are both jealous."

Randolph looked down and Hollings looked away before he snapped

"Yeah that's something alright. I can't even sleep at night because I feel so trapped."

Paschal sighed "I know how you feel, I think I died too when my mama went away,"

"Tell me about it, that was the worst day of my life. I think about her every day."

"What about the woman Hollings? Did she quit or did you leave her?"

"Call me James you Yankee scum and trust me you're not going to like that story either!"

15

Philomene had bodies to heal and souls to aid the rest of the afternoon

The line was getting really long so she told the men she'd see them soon

By that time they didn't mind for Hollings and Randolph were without care

They had found two things by which to bond and talked as they strolled through Jackson Square

Amidst flower pots along the Rue de Chartres, Hollings shared all of his reasons

Randolph overtly analyzed and discreetly criticized as he appraised the statues of the four seasons

Of financial losses, two dead sons and a wife he did most woefully lament

For the infants torn from their mother's breast at Clavijo plantation, he never did repent

He said "My father's heart beat for 100 years, but in 1802 his smile went away,"

"That was the year his cousins were massacred in Saint Domingue."

"Barbares!" was the last word a survivor said his childhood playmate spoke

Before he watched his six year old daughter hacked to pieces after being choked

"I know you hate to hear it but that's why he worked Niggers until they dropped,"

"He taught me they are all potential *Louvertures that would like to see my neck chopped."

* Toussaint Louverture (1743 –1803), was one of the leaders of the Haitian Revolution.

16

They dined at a fine restaurant on St. Louis Street before the spirits began to beckon

Not the disembodied kind but the ones that smelled of rye and caused one to regret and reckon

At the Tavern, men spoke of days that once were or they believe should have been

In that frame of mind everyone opined before a skull cracked beneath a bottle of gin

Paschal and Hollings were curious but were certainly not men of low taste

It was more than clear that this atmosphere was beneath them -- swallow it man and let's make haste!

For both men, the transition from sobriety was the most delicious feeling

A brown skinned woman suddenly stopped in front of Hollings, her lips were the most appealing

"Good evening loop de loo, how do you do?" She asked as she smoothed down her hair.

"When there's whiskey dreams are possible again, what brings you out from your lair?"

She looked at Paschal up and down, "You're so rude not to introduce me to this tall handsome fella,

I have about five names on any given night but you can call me Bella."

"Pleased to meet you, Dr. Randolph is what the world calls me but I call myself the Rosicrucian."

Bella laughed, "I don't know what that last word is but a doctor suits me fine,"

Hollings slapped Paschal on the back, "He'll come see you about nine."

17

Paschal watched Bella strut and asked, "Who's that woman that let you talk to her that way?

She acts like one of those Parisian girls at the cabaret."

Hollings shook his head and said "That is no Parisian, you see she has no class,

The only thing that woman is good for is a piece of ass."

Paschal frowned and walked ahead, "I think you have mistaken my character sir,"

"I must meet the soul before a vaginal fold or my member won't even stir."

Hollings jogged ahead and laughed at what he found to be absurd

"You need a solemnity to fuck, what terrible luck! That's the saddest thing I've ever heard."

Paschal watched the woman look back at him in the distance shaking ruffles and fringe

Her ass was so juicy and her neck so long. "Perhaps just this once" he cringed.

"Way to go Doc, you better go after her and snatch her up quick,"

"Don't be cheap cuz the way she's looking tonight she can certainly have her pick."

Paschal said goodnight to his new friend and walked as fast he could

To rendezvous with a random whore? Even a rich one -- He wasn't sure if he should.

18

At the corner, Bella turned around and sized up the man, "You gonna show me a good time?"

"I'm a sex magician mademoiselle and I'm in my prime."

"Yeah I heard about the colored man hanging by Laveau's turning everybody on,"

"If you think one of those potions will work on me that's where you're wrong."

Bella turned away and began walking faster than before

"Be careful little mama, I'm not the kind of man to grovel or follow you to your door."

Bella turned back around with an angry face and plunged a finger into his chest.

"I like you city boy but I'm the wrong bitch to fuck with. I don't take no mess."

Paschal gently took her finger and placed it on his ear

"I'm going to make you scream so loud this bullshit is the last thing I'm probably going to hear."

Bella gasped and slapped his face before she sauntered along

Paschal clutched his cheek and moved his jaw, "Damn that girl is strong!"

"Come on honey don't be like that. Where do you live? Now I can't wait!"

"Hollings already said it you cocky fool, it's the number after eight."

19

There was a gas lantern flickering outside a townhouse painted powder blue

The amber glow and the berries in the foyer made him want her more too

"You trick your customers and had the nerve to lecture me about potions?"

Bella removed his coat and breathed near his throat, "do you wanna come in rivers or oceans?"

Paschal gazed into her eyes and grabbed her arm "I ain't no John so let's get it straight, tonight that garbage isn't part of the plot,"

Bella jerked away and said "It'll be whatever you want it to be, depending on how much money you got."

He reached in his pocket and showed her the thirty dollars he was prepared to spend

"You must be a doctor and a fine one too. You just got yourself a new best friend."

She reached for the bills and he held up his hand, "First tell me whose place is this?"

She stepped forward and took the money, "A satisfied customer bought it for me because I was such a good mistress."

"So, have you always worked independently or did you work in another space?"

Bella looked confused as she went up the stairs. "You're a mewing dog ain't ya city boy. Yeah it was that familiar type of place."

"I hope you like to bathe because I touch no chattes unless it's clean."

"When you open it up you're gonna say to me, Bella that's the prettiest one I've ever seen!"

20

Paschal got into the bed with his member erect and hard

That's when he noticed the Garden of Gethsemane in the courtyard

Bella came into the room fresh out the tub glistening and soaking wet

She lifted an eyebrow at the steeple before her, "Guess I don't need to ask if you're ready yet."

"See that's where you're wrong, if we did it now it we would ruin all the fun,

Come over here and let me show you how it's supposed to be done."

"I'll take a punch, a choke and if you like, I'll pour hot wax on your jewels,"

"Just don't pee on me or break the skin cuz that's against the rules."

"I am a creature of transcendental love, my dear. That kind of soul can provide only pleasure,

How could any man see your form and not worship such a treasure?"

Bella turned to the looking glass and stared at her reflection

No man had ever spoken to her that way, they only gave her their erection

"If it's okay with you before we start, can we sit for a while outside?

"All you know is abuse and boys in heat and now you're terrified."

21

Hours later, Bella wept as her body continued to shake

"Will you marry me Paschal, I swear to honor the vows we'd make,

I ain't never felt so alive, Let me make you breakfast honey,

Here's your thirty dollars, after what just happened I can't take your money."

The Doctor stroked his goatee and dipped a finger in the tears falling down her cheeks

Then he licked the salty water, closed his eyes and asked her not to speak

"I won't be quiet! I can't I say! Not with my soul on fire!

You're the first man that ever made me want to retire."

"The world doesn't smile at women like me but I'd rather eat than be lawful,"

"I was born free but poor so at twelve years old I began to work at a brothel."

"They treated me like less than a person so at sixteen I escaped to work for another,"

"Fortunately for me this new Madame treated me just like a mother."

"But that's all over now, trust me Paschal. Forget my sins and please let me in."

CHAPTER TWO

"Thus the mother-a mother while becoming so,
which all too few are – willed her child to be all she
was, all its father was- whom she loved with all her
heart-and yet more! – and the father willful, egotistic,
boastful, haughty, vain, proud, conceited, sensuous,
ambitious, dictatorial, intellectual, prodigal, unstable,
variable, imperative; all these as a result of birth in an
old and proud family; all these crystallized and
condensed, mingled and mixed in their son; it will
readily be understood that he came fairly by his
angularities, eccentricities, personal appearance, talent,
psychic and spiritual powers, his charm and ability to
direct and fit into position, among all manner of men,
kings as readily as beggars."

– P.B. RANDOLPH

1

I have only known authority without love

Since the day she left

Her spirit reached for me

After it escaped its frail, sickly prison

My tiny arms were outstretched as a luminous portal consumed my own

She didn't scream but I did

I've never stopped

They said grief or the devil had manufactured the monstrous vision

Thank you world

For now I know there is an author -- or two, I must seek

That old Jack in the box is all I possess from those sorrowful days

I play with him still, when I'm alone

Turning the handle --remembering those soft brown eyes

Cranking and remembering...turning and turning

The man inside is content in that dark, wooden box

Because he knows he's not real...

Then, POP! I force him out of his home

I want to see him do the dance with that painted smile that makes me laugh

So I laugh—for a moment—but something happens to me once he stops jiggling

Once he becomes content and still in the sun

He bores me, so I push him back down to watch him struggle again

Because it's funny to me, because I can, because I possess him

Because he was created for this

I asked my mother's ghost that stood behind me in the mirror one day, "How long will it take before that little man breaks?"

I knew when she didn't answer that she couldn't

It was a question for fate.

2

There was nothing like Louisiana Heat -- they called it Creole Fire

It was so familiar that it greeted her by name

Prompting her to rouge both lips and mind

Bella was a tender girl life had prepped, tanned and crusted

Don't cry, a toughened hide was for the best

She was conceived in a barn as her mother tried to fight

That's what she heard in the field

Her mouth had been stuffed with hay so no one would hear her screams

That's what she knew because it had happened to her too

Why couldn't he at least let her breathe during the rape? No one would have helped anyway

Bella got her period for the first time and was freed the same morning

Her master's favorite said Jesus blessed her for not telling anyone about his "kiddie fun"

That's what she heard in the field

Before she entered the wagon full of snorting hogs

Where they would all be taken to the city to be ravaged by hungry carnivores

"Bye bye Papa," she mouthed as her father watched her roll away

He raised his left nub high in the air with happy tears in his eyes

Sure his daughter would be on her back most of the time but at least she would earn her own way

Her mother had been sold years ago -somewhere- to the highest bidder

She was forced to breed four children with her brother that had been sold two winters before -- because they were advertised in the paper as "undiluted sturdy Congo"

No, Mama would never know how it felt to be even kind of a person or get paid for hard work

Bella had it good

We all have it good.

Who cares if you're miserable? As long as it's the kind of misery that pays

Reflection is sorrow's lady in waiting

Don't serve her by looking at anything.

Mirrors are for applying rouge

Nothing more and nothing less

That's what the Creole fire said to Bella every day.

3

What does it mean to be civilized?

Where is that line between man and beast?

Was it speech? Or the ability to contemplate and excuse?

James loved being asked those questions because he knew the answer

It wasn't speech, for even birds squawk, caw and tweet

It wasn't the ability to ponder, for even a dog has its daydreams

It wasn't the power to justify or excuse either because well…

Fools are ubiquitous.

"So what is it James? Tell me what makes us human,"

His father walked with his hands in his pockets every time they strolled along the oak tree lined path

The man enjoyed reading more than anything else and even in his parlour, he kept at least one hand in his pocket

"Well, I guess the answer would be that for a people to be considered civilized they must have a civilization. Is that right?"

His father let out a hearty laugh and patted his son's wooly head "Son, you're as quick as a whip!"

The boy beamed with pride. "I think I'm quicker than that but it all depends on whose holding it right Pa?"

James Hollings Sr. smiled, "You're a good boy Jim, I hope you understand why I told you this. But you're still young so let me explain…"

It was a memorable moment on which his character was built

Though he could not recall every brick of its construction

Only a few words, quips and phrases managed to survive the erosion of time

But they were stronger than mud and straw, for those bricks had been fortified with blood, his blood, and baked under the sun of self-abasement

The strongest sun of all

Sometimes what his father said about Negroes bothered him but not because he cared about Negroes

No, that's not what bothered Junior at all

It was the reminder that he was always expected to care because of the way he looked. His father and his father before him also had that problem

His slaves would look at him with ten times more hate than they looked at the whites

As if they expected any profit man to be more moral than the next

Even the chickens know it matters not who eats them or why

They have the same awesome fear of all and for this they are wise

None is more foolish than they who propose impossible equations seeking a viable answer

That will never come

Lincoln and Lee clearly could not perceive what he has known since the age of thirteen

The difference between beast and man.

4

Is your mother home? No. Okay, then I'll come back later when she gets back

Rage. She knows how to peel, boil, pick and fix things too.

It didn't bother Euchariste none to live in their mother's shadow but it sure bothered Philomene

Marie LaVeau, Marie LaVeau, Marie LaVeau.

Philomene was tired. As is anyone with something to say that can't find an ear to listen.

That's why she has to do things differently than Marie LaVeau

Big and bombastic!

Red ruffles

Did ya see that yellow snake wrapped around her head like that?

Cussing on Sunday

She might even do a big job for you if you know how to ask!

We'll all die someday. Some of us deserve to go sooner

Is it really her sporting house? I thought she was Catholic?

The Lord and the Lwas told her twas' fine

Philomene wanted the mayor to send his carriage for her too

She wanted the governor's wife to trust her implicitly with her most intimate secrets as well

To those that say her gris-gris was not as powerful as Marie LaVeau -- pouah!

"Let that spit run down your face real nice and slow," she'd say.

They wouldn't dare retaliate!

But not because they respected her as much as they feared…

Marie LaVeau.

5

It was a Tuesday.

The first time she heard of "the Voodoo Queen of New Orleans"

Madame Marie, now in her sixties, sat in the second pew at St. Louis Cathedral

Praying to understand and to be understood

She touched the edge of the light blue fichu that covered her shoulders

It was the same one she wore almost forty years ago

Only now the color had faded a bit and the pink satin bow that held it together was gone

Still, it was her coronation robe and a voluminous red *tignon, was her crown

The *calas lady, the one with the deep voice, that walked with her hands on her hips was the one to tell her first

"Pssst, she said. Do you know what the Whites are sayin about you?"

Marie was tired after standing on her feet all day

But there was no such thing as being too tired to hear what the whites had to say

Marie pressed a coin into the woman's palm and took a fritter from her basket

"You root that man that wasn't payin that missy no mind, now theys gettin married!"

Marie stopped chewing. "You mean Selina Picard?"

"That's the one! That dried up stick she was pinin over made a turnabout the day after you left."

Marie laughed and took another fritter. "So, what they sayin now?"

"My baby say they callin you a voodoo queen or somethin."

"What's that?" Marie asked.

"I dunno," the woman shrugged.

"Well that's the stupidest thing I've ever heard. I'm just glad it worked, now she'll pay me that ten dollars so I can get some new shoes."

The calas lady placed a firm hand on her shoulder. "Stupid or not, if White folks say yous a Voodoo Queen then that's whatcha are. As long as dey happy it don matter no way. But if you don't do what they spect you already know they'll take away everything from ya. Heah?"

Marie smiled when she thought of that sweet old woman

She got up and lit a candle for her and sat back down

The flame danced…yes, that sweet old woman has been gone a long time now

It was a Tuesday, the year of our lord eighteen twenty six

When her role in life was re-cast as a villain or a saint

Depending on who stood to gain or lose by her playing either part

One hundred successful workings for coloreds made her respected but all it took was one lovesick white teenager with the right last name to make her a Queen

Marie looked at Jesus' hands. The nails.

Her hands had ached that day, that Tuesday, from making dozens of ringlets all afternoon

She was the best hairdresser in New Orleans

Marie LaVeau could turn a homely gal into the belle of the ball with just a few pins

A pretty girl? Oh, she could turn her into a Goddess!

With just the right suggestion for a feather, comb or Apollo knot placed just so…

Respected and trusted among her people

She made the impossible happen by saying the right thing to the right forces

Commanding doors to other realms to fly open with no effort

But so did Selina Picard

In fact they were no different at all

Marie rose and smiled before the cross

Merci Jesus et Notre Dame du Prompt Secours.

*Tignons are headcoverings that were required by law for women of color to wear.

*Calas are deep fried rice dumplings that were primarily sold by Black women in the 19th century.

6

Bella won't leave because of the way I love her

She runs her fingers through my hair and embraces me

Even if my back is turned, which it often is

There is nothing to say when all possibilities speak to me

Sometimes all at once

The horrors and the joys are inexplicable even for me

A man of words, unable to please even himself

Because the sun shines and thunderstorms rage, if I'm awake, simultaneously

Bella undresses in front of me as I smoke hashish

She wants me to want her as bad as I want myself

As voraciously as I want to be wanted by eternity

If I figure it all out, if I could just get it right I will always be welcome

Wherever I go, in the cosmos

"You smell good baby, of course you're beautiful..." I say.

I think of how I wish it was Philomene doing this dance of enticement

44

But there would be no need for red bows capturing her nipples to be undone with my teeth

I try not to look at the desk while she dances, I could write a good treatise now on the futility of literal seduction – at least for men of a certain degree

Philomene would do a different dance to keep me inspired

One that I'd never see but never cease to feel unless I was released

I am no lesser man that fears such an engulfment by woman because it is —to me—

The sweetest kiss.

There is a strong breeze tonight that blew out two of the candles

It sent Bella's hair flying all over the place

I am high and ascending ever upward until there is nowhere else to go but down or around…

"That's enough" I told her, gesturing with my finger for her to come closer

She couldn't wait for me to show her the stars again but I could see by the look in her eyes that she knew not her heavenly host

Was there anything worth knowing though?

Of course, I suppose

I am a doctor in the highest sense

A doctor of the souls of men.

7

To be in love for the first time must be what death is like to the recently deceased

It's probably all fear, confusion, relief and constantly wondering what's going to happen next

Would you be rewarded or damned?

Would you be guided or lost?

Would you be able to effectively state your case for why you were deserving of the absolute best?

And if not,

Was there a guarantee you would have another chance at bliss if you missed it?

Bella never expected to feel joy from a man's touch, much less a sense of peace from merely a glance

It was the worst thing and the best thing that could have ever happened to a heart burdened by so much pain

The best because it showed her that life had not forgotten her

And the worst because it would be confirmation that it had forgotten her once more

Bella prepared a meal for the doctor every evening since that first night

She wasn't angry if he didn't show up as long as he eventually did

And she knew because he was broken...over something...that he would

It didn't matter if he was in love or distracted by someone else

Yes, if there was anything Bella understood, it was men

She was paid well to know their ways and moods like their women couldn't

Bella also knew that Paschal would never be her man or anyone else's whether he was married or not

Some men were funny that way and she was glad he was one of them

Now she would never waste her time being jealous of anyone else

No, she could never weep over a turtle man that carried his home with him and whose shell would never be big enough for two

But Bella loved him and hoped she would at least be allowed to sit next to, polish or stroke that mighty shell of the most beautiful man she ever met

Dinner was getting cold but her desire for Paschal never would

It was something about the way he dreamed that made her want to dream that way too

She drank the elixirs he prepared hoping whatever was in it could make her understand all those pretty things he said

When she did that, the doctor just stared through her from across the room and went back home inside his skull where no one could reach him

How could an obsession with someone happen so quickly? So completely? She wondered as she ate alone.

Again.

8

Hollings was a simple man that enjoyed life's simple pleasures

A good book, melancholic piano sonatas, absinthe and vain nostalgia

How many of his tears had watered the idealistic notions of someone else's past?

He could not say, for if it were quantified... it would be a tributary flowing into a vast lake of impossibilities

Hollings wanted to grow old with a sense of clarity as his crutch

He wanted familiar ways and familiar days

Change was never his forte

Hollings had to sell nineteen of his best slaves to cover his debts

Including Lucie

She worked in the house and bore him two children

Two girls that looked just like their Mama, ugly as sin but somehow, they managed to compose a pretty smile

But beauty wasn't why Hollings wanted Lucie back

He missed the way her misery made him feel

Breaking her was for him, an unparalleled joy beyond comprehension

One time, he dangled her baby over a pit of hungry dogs

Another time he had her man broken by the overseer before he opened his throat

She tried to comfort her man as he bled out with his face in the dust

No need. The back of a shovel sure does make a mess of things but at least it was finished

Hollings was a gentleman through and through but it was just something about Lucie

He couldn't do anything like that to anyone else but her

Lucie released something…she made him feel so good

He had to get her back now that money wasn't so tight

Before Lincoln did his awful deed. But it didn't matter he'd shoot her before he'd ever see her happy and free

Her frown was his redemption, her pain was a balm for his own

Hollings begged every root worker in town to help him get her back but they refused

Philomene was the only one that said "Maybe, one day."

No, Lucie could not be allowed to escape and he would do anything to make it so

Including condemn his soul.

9

Philomene kissed her husband and daughter as they slept

Their tickle fight had been raucous, loud and exhausted them both

Her man was good to her, just as her father had been to her mother

And not just because of that

No, he was genuinely in love with Philomene

She could tell by the way he kissed her forehead and brushed her hair

Men don't do things like that when they're just fond of you

Mama wasn't feeling so good that morning so Philomene took on her clients

It had been a rough day

Chasing kids, cooking dinner, rubbing her husband's back, anointing this and that

But she had a good life compared to most

She had friends, family and a thriving business

Philomene sighed, rubbed her palms on her gingham apron and sat outside

Four fireflies circled and flashed their lights near her feet

"Yeah," she said, "I do want something new to see."

She had never left Louisiana and until he came she never wanted to

The good Dr. Randolph carried the world in his eyes

Both its joys and the havoc wreaked on him by its surprises

He read her poetry in French and wondered what it'd be like to accompany him to the Tuileries for tea with Napoleon

That was his friend you know,

But that was a long way from home, perhaps too far

And even if it wasn't, she couldn't leave Emile and the baby

Her and Paschal waltzing beneath glittering chandeliers? That's insane!

10

Everyone is arrogant because everyone has a plan

Everyone is pompous because everyone makes predictions

There is nothing prouder than assuming you will see the next sunrise

Every time you say later...you strut

Every time you say tomorrow...you strut

Every time you say never...you strut

Humility is recognition that life could be no other way

So, you love your assumptions with all of your heart

Instead of patting their cheeks condescendingly

If you want it to rain, tug on a single drop in a cloud somewhere high above your head that might like to meet you

Then you convince that drop to tell the others to come too because it sure is fine down below

If you ask the raindrops the way they like to be talked to, they'll go

They are no different than you.

Even if the sun is shining as bright as can be, always carry an umbrella if you asked for rain

It will come because the drops that fall believe in later, tomorrow and never too

That's why the rain you call must be stored in jars

It's called 'yes water' because it came by request

And now that those friendly drops are there

Let them tell your garden, your neighbors, your lovers and your friends

'No' is not said to humble servants of God

Even if for a while that's the way it seems to be

If it isn't the rain than it might be the leaf of a tree

That is one of the secrets of conjure.

"It's the path of will and ways." said Madame Marie.

11

A humpback offered me a bottle of tafia as I was crossing the street

I looked at the camel man, then at the label-less bottle

I tried to shoo them both away

He asked me why I didn't buy his liquor

I told him "I don't drink cheap."

I kept walking briskly toward Lake Pontchartrain

The camel man moved that gnarled twisted body faster than I imagined

He blocked my path. His hair covered one eye.

"My rum ain't cheap because I ain't, Breedlove's the name."

I tipped my hat, apologized and paid the man

That's what he was, a man. I had to compensate him for my offense

But the liquor was still cheap

I drank the fermented cane juice like it was a matter of life and death

Now I'm drunk with a corseted smile

The water beckoned to me all day

To extinguish the inferno in my breast

Here I am at the waterfront, alone

She asked me why I burned bridges again

And an image of a bridge aflame suddenly appeared

It burned proud and bright

My mind's eye teared at the sight of its beauty

They didn't want me to share what I had clearly seen

They were mad about my position on slavery

Should objects in full view not be deemed an exhibition?

To you or to me?

Literate subordinates grasping for democracy's scraps from their high chairs

A pitiful sight indeed

Turn up your quasi aquiline noses! I stand with America and the freedmen

Rise Creole fire…take everything away

I shall rub my face with the ashes of their hatred like a reverent Hindoo

The truth is all I need.

12

He was one of her regulars

The pretty Sicilian with the curly hair

The son of the friendly man that owns the corner store

Bella dug her nails deep into his chest right before

Well, you know…

A white cat saw the whole thing this time

It just sat there watching them with those curious yellow eyes

They hadn't noticed it was there but Pietro didn't mind

After they finished catching their breath, he made shadow figures on the wall

His cigarette smoke spiraled toward the mouth of a shadow dog

"I gatti hanno sette spiriti" he said with a sigh

The Italian words were like a song

"What does that mean?" Bella asked.

"I said cats have seven spirits."

Bella watched Pietro playing with the cat in the mirror's reflection as she brushed her hair

"That's a notion, I always heard they have nine lives."

Pietro blew out three smoke rings

As precise and long lasting as his passion for anything but art and acts of love

He fixed his eyes on hers, "If you have seven ways to breathe one life is enough."

Bella walked over to him and tenderly touched his face

"This is the last time we will ever meet like this."

The white cat scampered away...

It made a grand leap and landed in the garden

At the same time a tear fell from Pietro's eye

"You've always been my favorite but I'm in love."

Pietro's silence

A silence that revealed he had taken his feelings for her way too far

Bella passed him his trousers and what had become his mourning coat

Pietro walked to the door but his hand froze on the knob

He traced the features of the bronze lion that jutted forth above the doorknob

"You have inspired the best idea I've ever had." he said without turning around

"But everything you make is nice."

Pietro walked out

Bella watched him walking down the street

Happy to have met him but not sorry he was gone

"I'm glad I did not interrupt that beautiful scene."

Bella was stunned to find Paschal standing in the doorway

In his arms, was the white cat

Bella shook her head, "It wasn't beautiful, it was sad."

"But the wall paper maker expressed how badly he wanted many ways to see."

Bella's eyes grew wide with surprise

Was she impressed or frozen in fear?

Bella's eyes pleaded for the answer from the white cat

Paschal smirked and walked away

And when she finally melted

The sound of a contented purr filled the air.

13

Negroes reading was a bad idea, Hollings told Paschal

For it would seed flowers of purpose that would never fully grace the light

Instead the race of loathly ladies would only anxiously await the knight that could never truly love her

Never embrace her, except to forcefully have his way

By deception or pain

Rash boons only sell melons in winter

Idealism is a canker on the lip of a rational man, a realistic man, an honest man

The northerner did not listen to him, nor to any of them

The doctor of course, always knew best

"Urbanity caused a terrible deafness." James' father used to say.

But the New Yorker suffered the worst case of self-righteous rot

Now his friend was a principal of peasants

Fulfilling the principles of fools

What school could possibly aid a beast of burden with a burden so heavy it must sing just to stand?

With a will so eroded by sensuosity that even if the burden was lifted

It could not stand on its own

The doctor did not speak of men today at Café du Monde but of the troglodytes of yesteryear

Such obtuse emanations were unceasing from a dreamer's mind

"A protoype of humanity's glory," Paschal smiled.

The men sipped coffee blended with chicory

Dr. Randolph stared at the awning of green and white stripes, "These troglodytes were the progenitors of Negroes…the stupid kind."

Hollings cleared his throat. "So, if you know that is the essence of your students than why do you try?"

"Because I have seen the impossible become commonplace too many times before my eyes."

Hollings shrugged. "Atlas must bear the weight of the heavens or the world collapses."

Beignets.

So warm and sweet.

Let's eat them in peace, for a while.

14

So the rumor is true, thought Philomene

Bella was fucking her Dr. Randolph!

I mean, she had a husband already

But Paschal remained perfect because he hadn't disappointed her yet

He came by the other day to treat the brothel mirrors

All long limbs and swag

Some say his lips are too thin for his face --- but to her, that was one fine man

"Put three mirrors on the left, five on the right and seven atop in each room after I'm done,"

Then he rubbed them down with a silk cloth, fed em and sprayed em with rum

He held a cigar to her lips and told her to give it a lick before it was lit

Their intentions were in the Smoke and it finished off the reflecting glass real nice

It made sweet daddy fall into a trance

So together, they danced

Their spirits came, she heard hers and his

They told her what they both needed to do but before she could say a thing

The good doctor Randolph said "I love you too."

Philomene let the room spin as he kissed her neck

She didn't care that his eyes showed nothing but white

That's how she looked too

There they were trickin mirrors

Tempting destiny

Risking Sanity

Birth Life and death,

The Senses

Perfection.

15

Randolph said, "I used to believe in the Lord but now I only believe in one God."

Madame Marie could smell Paschal's breath--- sweetened by brandy milk punch

She clutched a pink and green beaded rosary, the same colors as her dress

There was sawdust on his shoes from all the grindin they'd done

Precious will be the day when souls like his proliferate

But not too much

The world would become too heavy to spin and too light to please them

"Have some tea," said the aging priestess to her perpetually agonized guest

She folded her arms and watched him as he drank

He sipped it and coughed before taking a little more

"You ain't gonna ask what's in that cup?"

Dr. Randolph smiled, gulped it down and stretched out his palm

She said "I don't see nothing but the best kind of trouble."

He lifted a brow and stroked his mustache, "How?"

Madame Marie traced the star on his fame line and sighed

"The world fears the fearless but after death, they worship the bones."

Paschal kissed his palm and placed it tenderly over his heart

She wasn't sure if out of pride or pain

Madame stretched out her palm before him -- "You're not the only one."

"Hu-Ra! Two dead Gods are better than none!"

She sucked her teeth and looked out of the window

"I'm only going to tell you once to leave my child alone."

Dr. Randolph's smile faded faster than a cynic with a positive thought

"But veuve Glapion, Philomene and I are only friends,"

"I like you doctor, I really do but my child is in danger messin round the likes of you."

Dr. Randolph arose and took his hat from the hook.

"Your request is out of place and therefore must be denied. So with that Madame, I bid you goodbye."

She turned around with her eyebrows joined and pointed a finger at his chest

Paschal smiled, "I won't leave her alone on my own, so go ahead, do your best."

Chapter Three

"Every genius is ticketed for misery in this life; for
theirs is but an angular, one sided, painful
development. A few advantages are purchased at an
enormous cost. A short, brilliant, erratic career, more
kicks than praises; more flattering leeches than fast
friends; rich and joyous today, houseless and suffering
the pangs of hell tomorrow; understood by God
alone; seldom loved till dead; the victims of viciously
minded men, and the solitary pillars of life. Genius is
a bright bauble, but a dangerous possession;
invariably open to two worlds. They are assaulted,
coaxed, flattered, led captive on all sides through their
affectionate nature. Rest comes to them only with
death; and peace comes only through the knowledge
of having done their best. They are compelled to train
all their previously neglected facilities to something
like harmony with those few wherewith they startled
the world."

– P.B. RANDOLPH

1

I taught a little Negro girl a great secret today

Her name is Prevail St. James

A dark-skinned cutie --- she's nine or perhaps a little older than ten

I sit in my room writing about her now with joy and confusion in tow

I'm happy to have met such a brilliant child yet I have abandoned my own

Why did I leave my wife with only demands for inconsistencies' pardon?

I am truly my father's son

But when the voice of regret extends from note to frequency

That is mother

Then -- when I can sit with guilt no longer

My excuses play golden harps

After the comforting recitation of man's ancient sermon of faultlessness

I may begin again unseeing what I have been clearly shown

That is the spirit of mercy -- I believe

And to that spirit I raise my cup high before I let the dead imbibe

Excuses have saved me once more -- as do all false prophets of mysterious forces that are permitted to cause confusion

Prevail St. James

A beautiful name and mental state that is

We will be teacher and pupil for as long as I live.

2

Bella went away for a few days to see the lady of Baton Rouge

The lady was part Indian they said, with a wide gap between her teeth

Folks also told her she was crazy cuz of all those mounds she'd make in her backyard

She never explained what they were to anyone

But women went to see her anyway

Crazy or not, they would see anyone that could make their man stay

You see, Eliza Pelfrey made a deal with the four sisters of Lake Maurepas

Those ladies poured into old Maurepas and kept the water fresh

And those big cypress stumps were the pillars of Solomon's temple

You could go to them for advice when morals frayed

Her house almost touched the water because she loved it so much

The lady had long white hair that gleamed in the sunrise

It was thinner than the strings of moss that hung above her crown

She watched Bella wash Paschal's new cravats in the holy water

Two of the ties were even kissed by a whisker fish

The old woman smiled, "Did you see that blessing? Those are the two you should give him as a gift."

When the sky became as blue as the hydrangeas on the porch they went inside to pray

But not like you did in church, the lady did it another way

Nothing they said about Eliza Pelfrey was true except who her grandma was and how she looked

Those web weavers feared how she pulverized hot love to make it fitting and wise

"All they understand is the noon of everything," she said,

"And that's why joy never comes."

Bella begged lady to make Paschal love her forever

"Do you think I control the spirits of Lake Maurepas?" The old woman asked.

Bella looked into lady's eyes but then -- she had to look away

Where had the sudden pain in them come from? Surely there must be some mistake

Eliza Pelfrey shook her head and walked toward the water's edge

She explained only slaves had a master but you could always persuade a friend.

3

Dear Brother,

I found a letter here from you, one from Providence and one from Jacob. It was yours I opened first. I was so happy that you could still send a letter through. I hasten to inform you of the death of my father in law, may the lord rest his soul. I curse the Union for causing this hideous war that made me a widow so young. Now we have lost two! It would have broken Richard's heart that his father died shivering in a ditch wrapped in a rubber coat. There is so much death and destruction I scarcely know what to do. I know how you feel about missing your Lucie, three of my servants left me too.

The mosquitos are meaner than they have ever been but I am still in better health than usual. Oh how I miss when we were children! Before life became so complicated and hard. Remember when I used to refuse to eat peaches unless I was wearing my favorite dress? You got so mad but father just laughed and laughed. Still, you would not take a bite without me, it's that kind of loyalty you never forget.

Carol is packing for New Orleans now. I suffer terrible fears that the Union will eventually destroy my childhood home. Please be there James, Please be alive and well when I get there for I don't know what I would do if you weren't. Instead of balls all I

attend now are funerals. I do not think I could bear another, least not yours. I am sorry for exhibiting such forthright gloom but I know as soon as I see your face and mother's tree my disposition will improve. I love you.

Sincerely, Sadie

4

Every whore in New Orleans visited Dr. Randolph's apothecary, including Philomene's

They gossiped about the six paneled coromandel made of lacquer, mother of pearl, tortoiseshell and gold---all crunched up in that tiny room

The doctor claimed it was a gift from a rich china man he saved but of any other details he said little else

All the rich white johns saw him before they went to the sporting house for a boost

That colored man is brilliant they cried, "He can get you hard as a rock without a congestor, a splint or a cat o' nine tails whip."

From the ladies, she had never heard such sounds emit!

Her purse fattened like a hog a fortnight before the kill

But still -- Philomene fumed

She wanted to know what was in those tonics and inside him too

To that request he said he had no cures for cough, cold or nosy curiosity

He would not tell her the ingredients but happily revealed what the elixir for prostitutes was

Dr. Randolph's voice went deep when he said, if a man does not love a woman when he beds her than she is both whore and prey

The situation is worse, he continued, when love is claimed. So, the john she calls lover or husband consumes a piece of her soul for free and she's not even paid

Philomene sniffed the tonic he called 'Répulsif Vampire' for women like the ones she employed

Her head jerked back -- it was red, strong and bittersweet

Dr. Randolph winked at her as she removed the cork from the next bottle

The elixir to soothe the uncompensated whores -- the betrothed and betrayed 'Chevalerie liquide' or Liquid Chivalry was that one's name

Philomene lit a cigarette with her left hand and the other arm akimbo

That's all well and good for them. But where's the tonic for women that no longer love their man but must still remain?

5

I pray to you sweet Saint Gengulphus

I ask you to touch this water with your staff and make it holy

Get all up in it Saint Gengulphus!

You know how it feels to have the woman you love run around on you

Don't let that happen to Monsieur Legendre, he's a good man

Protect that married home dear Saint

Protect my grandchildren from the shame of their mother's lust

I don't want you to hurt my child -- she's just confused that's all

She knows deep down that the man she wants ain't gonna stay anyhow

Increase her sight Saint Gengulphus, I don't want her to burn in hell like your wife

Please, please, please God don't take my baby away to New York

She'll only get thrown away

Bless this cloth, this palm branch, this cross and dagger too

When the water turns as red as this cloth after the moon is full its martyr's blood

And then that man won't be able to see my baby, let alone come close

The candle will stay lit.

*Saint Gengulphus (died 760 AD), was a Burgundian courtier/hermit and Christian martyr. He is invoked against adultery and to repair difficult marriages.

6

I have been labelled an infidel

A disbeliever in the reality of God

How could that be when that is all I live for?

How could that be when I have sacrificed every material comfort and the love of mortal men to speak the truth?

*Mr. Howard has slit the throats of Seminole women and children with his own hands!

Yet, I am the one divorced from benevolent humanity

Yet, I am the one that writhes between the crack of Satan's brimstone

Yet, I am the one that eternal peace shall mock and shun with a heavy brow

How long must the black man be slandered by slime and accused by myth?

It is true, I said Jesus is not God

It might not have been wise when asking for funding from missionaries -- but I was asked my opinion on the matter!

God is electricity, is motion and light

Does not the portrayal of auric fields surrounding the head of saints illustrate this?

Does not the storm of love's climax reveal the secret of all beginnings?

Do not the discoveries of Thales, Galvani or Volta show you nothing more?

I suppose not, it would probably be asking too much to consider the thoughts of this White Crow

That's what he called me you know --

Mr. Howard called *me* --a rarity for being a deviation from the faithful--black--flock

I, the one who lives as a particle of the deific brain and celebrates this great, pulsating mass rather than merely singing its praises

I and people like me --We are the odd ones

The scorned ones

The wind gust behind the backs of good men that will eventually lead them to their fall

It never occurs to them that what they manifest with every waking breath has condemned them all

The child-killers, brain washers and great manipulators say I am a libel upon my race

That I am to be branded so whenever anyone looks upon my face

What kind of brand do you suggest may I ask? Perhaps an R on my forehead like a runaway slave?

Or how about a more personalized stamp?

Whatever you choose, please do it quickly

So the libels might graze together freely on the open range -- before you eat your steak

But you are not entirely wrong sir, I am as lost as lost can be

I am unable to find my way out of the deceptive maze called Northern morals and liberality

I have wronged you Hollings and General Lee!

If consistency is blessed by God than your foreheads have been kissed

For the vainglory of the friends of Blacks wielding invisible chains and whips receive only God's spit

Forgive my terrible knees that stiffen when asked to bend

Pardon my unwillingness to teach how to be court jesters and other kinds of fools

It's good to know no libels like me will ever be produced at your *Negro normal schools.

* Oliver Otis Howard (1830 – 1909) was an Indian fighter and a Union general. He was also the founder and first president of Howard University, a historically Black college in Washington DC.

*A normal school was an institution created to train prospective teachers according to the states' standards. Blacks had to attend separate normal schools due to segregation laws.

7

Lady was the mother Bella never had

She was the friend of none so she could be a friend to all

And because of her power, she was a woman time never met

Eliza ate boiled peanuts as she gently placed empty eggshells on a mound

Bella filled them with soda bread that had an x on the top and pushed them down

When Bella asked her why they were doing it, Eliza Pelfrey let out a sigh

"You asked for a man to be fixed to stay."

"There ain't no human voice soft enough to convince a man that wants to leave not to go away."

The moonlight hit the shells and Bella closed her eyes

She could feel Paschal's warm embrace

As soon as Bella's eyes opened, Eliza dangled a red string in front of her face

The most absurd question had just escaped her lips

"Are you sure you want him this bad?" she quipped.

There was only one thing in the world she wanted more than the Rosicrucian

It was only one other thing that moved her to the core

Permanence

Dear sweet permanence

Who to all that are happy -- is the biggest whore.

Eliza drank muscadine wine and spoke of not writing checks her ass couldn't cash well into the night

She smirked as the old woman worked that red string like a spider

But that was only what people like Bella saw

To the old woman it was a vein upon which the fairies could run

They would transport Bella's wishes upon that bridge that connected Paschal's ears and heart

It was their wedding day because Lady helped her tie the knot

After a dab of vervain oil the mighty link Eliza called a tafo, was fastened around Bella's waist

"Now you got your lawyers to plead your case but they have a price."

The blushing bride beamed with pride as she was showered with more warnings than rice.

8

Sadie was a dumb, clumsy child with bad breath and a stutter

She ran wild and got them in trouble more times than he could count —but still her brother loved her

The speech problem began after their mother went to heaven

It was the hottest summer anyone could remember -- the body was rotting quickly

And some said that Sadie's voice got stunted by the stench

That made no sense to James because he never smelled a thing

All he perceived was the emptiness of an unfathomable loss

Sadie cried because she didn't like the way they did their mother's hair

She shouted at the service "Why did you put that curl there!"

Sadie was always particular about such things -- and clothes

Hollings smiled as he remembered when she said "Jjjjjust bbbecause I sssound stupid doesn't mean I can't llllloook smart."

She came up with pretty new designs all the time

It wasn't long before she became famous and people came to see her from far and wide

Father only tolerated so much attention because his wife would have approved

James tolerated it because his sister promised to banish combinations of blue and yellow from all of her shows

They were the colors of their mother's favorite dress --- the dress she was buried in

Their aunt's eyes began to roll to the back of her head when she saw her baby sister lying there and collapsed in grief

"Only Negroes mourned in such a flagrant way," Father whispered to James in between gritted teeth.

Sadie kept smoothing down her mother's dress to make sure she looked as neat as can be

The child even designed new clothes for their slaves

They had to switch back when she made them look so good that a few managed to escape

She raged at the sight of jean cloth anywhere near the house

The cook would come running after the offender waving a giant wooden spoon

"Git on outta heah wit dem clothes on boy! You know Ms. Sadie's way!"

The cook's voice echoed in James' ears as his sister twirled her parasol down the great oak path

It had been a few years

Her eyes were still as green as the leaves on the trees

Unlike him, she came out with hardly a hint of the family's stain except for those big pink lips

Besides that flaw, she was almost as perfect as their mother

She was a business woman now too, with a thriving plantation

There existed no prouder brother.

9

It had been a long time since Dr. Randolph stopped by

Philomene saw him tilt his hat in her direction from outside Betsy's store

Did he get tired of waiting for her or was there something more?

Philomene knew the answer before she asked

It had to be mama's doing

She was always getting in the way of something she wanted!

She was always trying to fix her life to suit her taste!

Philomene spun around the room

On each wall there was the image of a saint

Which one of you took chicken, coffee or cake?

Saint Peter shook his head

Saint Joseph did nothing but sleep

Saint Anthony said nothing and our lady of sorrows--- just continued to weep

Philomene felt the room getting hotter or was it rage?

Why had she been born to Marie Catherine Laveau?

When would she escape her shadow and cage?

Philomene burst through her mother's door

She pushed everyone out of the way

An old man lost his footing and fell on the floor

Dr. Randolph wasn't her man or nothing but she liked the way he showed her things

Philomene liked that he had something to show,

He was like no one she had ever seen

And she wanted a piece

But of what?

Men always thought good lovin was the secret to her heart

But for Philomene that wasn't the key

She wasn't one of those women that get the Gede snake and start whining to Eliza Pelfrey

No, she was different. Not like the silly girls that paid that Irish witch!

She had to clean up many a stuck fellow that didn't know their dicks were in a ditch

Dr. Randolph was the only man that was really worth her time

How would she cope without his tonics, conversation and smile?

She didn't mean to knock anyone down

Philomene didn't see that cart flip over

It was passion that made petite Marie not see

It was desperation to keep a jewel she found that made her march on

To the home of a friend she ain't talk to in a long time

Her mother's sworn enemy -- Dr. John.

10

Madame Marie rushed home right away when she heard the news

Philomene had left her house in a state of fury with her fists all balled up

Some even say she spoke foul language as she passed St. Louis Cathedral

Her daughter committed a sin if she did that

Apparently, she despised her mother that much

Madame Marie closed the drapes, sat in her chair and wept

All she wanted to do was protect her baby from a bad end

Philomene was a mother too, why couldn't she understand?

There is no mother in the world that wouldn't do for her children if she could

If it was possible to stop a horse from trampling them in the road

There is no question that you should

Doctor Randolph was that horse

The kind that rather get shot down than stop the buck

The kind that blocks his blessings but blames it all on bad luck

Madame Marie thought of how many times she's seen people do that

Maybe hundreds in thirty years

They come to her all tired and worn not realizing it wasn't the evil eye that got um

But the weight of their own fears

Now the lines deepened around her eyes and mouth for the same reason

What would be said to her at the pearly gates, dear God?

Would her soul be forgiven for the mistakes she's made?

Father told her to give up her Voodoo ways and repent before it was too late

She kissed the clergyman's hand when he smiled at her

Despite her transgressions against the Lord of hosts

He kissed hers for never telling a single soul she protected him

From getting caught with the one he fornicated with most

"One day I will give it all up," she thought

And at that time, I will give up my soul to thee

But right now, I must do as I must

Because my baby needs me.

Chapter Four

"In New Orleans nothing is more common than for both men and women to employ the voudeaux to effect contact with loved or desired ones. I have never known a failure, albeit some experiments of acquaintances of mine were rather expensive."

– P.B. RANDOLPH

1

I am a sun for those that want to bask in my light and a moon for those that want to be inspired

Ever since my days at sea, I dreamed of being useful to someone -- because I never was

That's why I founded *Fraternitas Rosae Crucis six years ago

At every destination I travelled, I collected luminous threads and wove them with my own ideas

As the figureheads of all revolutions across time and space have done

I am a master

The first supreme grand master of a fraternity, that I believe, will one day be truly great

A fraternity that will nourish the speculative mind and fortify the souls of all that seek the iron of truth that once enters the blood, could never be removed

I have worked hard and I have made many, many regretful mistakes

Both personal and professional

Like most men, I have lied to myself more times than I care to count

About who I was, what I was, what I wanted or the real intent behind certain actions

But there is one thing I have never been -- is disloyal to me. A liar on occasion, yes, but never disloyal

Do I think I will be credited for all that I've done? Do I think that in one hundred years the Rosicrucians will remember me?

Unless this country, unless this consciousness, is very different than it is today -- I think not

The genius of no colored men will be recognized in full unless it is brutish or coarse

So that is my fate, a fate I have always known and resolved within myself before I even begun

If I had done otherwise, if I had become overwhelmed by the sorrow of that reality

I would not have written anything beyond a letter to a friend or lectured beyond the propriety of a child's bedtime

The world made me realize a long time ago that an extraordinary Black man must expect absolutely nothing

For the extraordinary colored person -- selflessness, humility and martyrdom are not some lofty virtues that better men of the other hue aspire to

But a requirement if one wishes to contribute anything that might live on for a thousand years

Or to be considered serious and beautiful.

---

*Fraternitas Rosae Crucis is a Rosicrucian fraternal organization founded by Paschal Beverly Randolph in 1858, and is the oldest Rosicrucian Order in the United States.

2

Bella entered Paschal's room like a burst of sunshine

But the doctor was not surprised -- he had fallen asleep again at his writing desk

Bella picked up one of the papers, being careful in case the ink wasn't yet dry

She read the part about martyrdom and sucked her teeth

Bella didn't like it when he talked like that

"Paschal, it's me. I'm back."

The man didn't awaken so the woman tugged his goatee

Paschal stirred once his lover began dotting kisses all over his face

Bella began to rub his back

Then his arms

Then his chest

Before she could reach what she wanted to rub next

He got up and walked away to look out of the window

"I missed you," he said.

Bella walked closer to him, "I missed you too. That's why I came here first. I haven't even been home yet."

The Doctor cleared his throat

He gazed out of the window at the green shutters and the pink ones

And all the others as far as he could see

Paschal's face looked as stern as a Carpetbagger

"Take off your clothes," he instructed.

Bella wanted to comply but she couldn't -- she was still wearing the tafo!

"I didn't come by for that."

Paschal walked over to the desk without taking his eyes from hers

He lit a cigarette and blew the smoke out in a long thin stream

Bella swallowed hard and began to sift through her bag

"I brought you something from Baton Rouge I thought you might like."

Paschal held up his hand for her to stop

"I said, take off your clothes!"

It was the first time Bella felt any fear of the normally soft spoken doctor

Paschal sat down at his writing desk to watch her undress

Bella shook as she placed the bag on the bed and removed her shoes

Then her hat, gloves and shawl

Then her chemise, corset cover and corset

Then her hoops

Pause

"Why'd you stop?" asked the doctor.

Bella felt like her stomach dropped to her feet -- "I can't, it's my woman's time."

"Keep going" he said between clenched teeth.

Bella slowly took off her pantalettes and stockings

Now she was completely nude in every way

Paschal stared at the knotted red cord around her waist

Then he blinked and looked at her

Bella wanted to scream as he approached

But she knew all too well that the best way to take a punch was to remain quiet --

And stand straight up.

Paschal's eyes were ablaze as helpless tears streamed down her face

They were nose to nose as he began to yank at the tafo

Until it finally snapped -- the hoodoo was broken -- and she wondered if her neck would be next

He hurriedly lifted up her leg and undid his trousers with his free hand

Then he kissed her softly and whispered "You didn't have to do all that."

3

Sadie had not been home a week before she insisted that her brother host an elaborate ball

"I want to see all of my friends and make new ones. I especially want to meet that eccentric doctor you told me about."

James sighed.

Balls weren't his style and even if they were he wasn't in the mood for one.

"What's the matter Jimmy? Don't tell me you've grown old and boring already!"

James flashed his sister an incredulous look. "Come on, when have I ever been boring?"

"Then what is it then? Is it money? Are you having money trouble Jimmy? You're not gambling again are you?"

"Mo té pe pa kasé mô labichud."

"What do you mean you can't break your habit? Do you want to end up poor, without anything nice? We don't know how to live like that James. Promise me neither of us will ever find out."

James put his sister's head on his shoulder and patted her hand. "The war may impoverish everyone. The whites too. Those goddamn Yankees are going to ruin us all."

Sadie slowly lifted her head and sat up straight.

James was always the optimistic one of the family. She had never heard him talk that way. It frightened her.

"The last time the ladies and I got together my friend Colleen spoke like that. Our husbands had just finished voting in a new member of the *Brown Fellowship Society. A nice fellow named John Claymore and then all of a sudden Colleen..."

Sadie sniffled and blinked her eyes real fast.

James placed a hand on her shoulder "What happened?"

"Colleen screamed and started ranting and raving. She said that the Blacks would kill us when they got free and the Yankees wouldn't stop them."

"Oh Sadie, I'm so sorry I upset you. I didn't mean to make you sad. Really I didn't."

Sadie patted her brother's cheek and eyeballed two slaves walking by.

James shouted for them to "git!" and turned back to his sister, "Why didn't you mention this in any of your letters?"

"Because I didn't want to upset you. I was ashamed because I know it was my fault Colleen went crazy."

Sadie sobbed into a handkerchief

She cried hard and long

Longer than someone with just a passing fear

"You told Colleen what happened to our aunt in Saint Domingue all those years ago, didn't you?"

Sadie shook her head. "I never forgot when father told us how they butchered our family James! How could anyone forget that? They must have been so scared!

And the children…oh lord all those beautiful children!"

James took his sister in his arms and rocked her like he used to when they were little

When a few pats on the back, soft words and a little candy could make the world right again

But those days were long gone -- they were all grown up now

Scared and scarred.

---

*The Brown Fellowship Society was a prestigious an all-male Funeral Society in Charleston, South Carolina that only admitted light skinned mulattos, quadroons and octoroons.

4

Dr. John told her he wasn't going to touch Dr. Randolph because he had already been fixed

"That old Bambara makes me so mad!" she thought,

He's just rich and comfortable now. He could have done something

All he said was that he saw dragonflies fluttering around his head

That's when Philomene left Dr. John's place in the same huff as when she came

It ain't nobody but that Eliza Pelfrey working those flittery things!

But who loved him that much to go to Baton Rouge?

It ain't nobody but that nasty ho Bella LaBranche!

Philomene slapped down those playing cards in order to see the whole picture

But there was nothing there

That dumb ole Jack just stared at her straight back

It pissed her off -- the way his big nose seemed to be sniffing the heart like that

But that didn't matter she didn't need to see it all because she knew enough

That's when Philomene ran to Dr. Randolph's place to let him know about the root put on him

She couldn't stop recollecting that day as she cleaned the house

Mr. Legendre and the baby went -- somewhere

And then Paschal did something she never saw a man do before

Yes, he surprised her once again!

When most men learn a love root been put on em, they get spittin mad

But when she asked that crazy Rosicrucian if he was vexed all he said was "Eh, just a tad."

He made a half inch measure hand gesture with his thumb and index finger when he said that

Philomene angrily blew hair out of her face as she aggressively scrubbed the floor

She got that stubborn grime in the corner nice and clean

When she imagined it was Bella's face

Why was she cleaning up for herself anyway?

That's right. That scrawny girl with the debt was sick.

What did he mean that passion should never be chastised if it had a noble heart?

"That bitch just wants a way out of laying on her back, like she's always done!"

"You think like that," he said with that deep, melodious voice.

Philomene laughed when she mimicked him out loud

Before she felt sad again because he wasn't there

Nor did he even care -- that she went out of her way to warn him

Philomene got up quickly and hastily scooped up her skirt

Merde! --Now there's water everywhere

She grabbed some old cloth out of the closet to clean it up

But instead she dropped to her knees in the dirty water

Jealousy was the best trick of all.

5

Madame Marie fed her granddaughter gumbo

As she tried to console her son-in law

People don't know how to mind their own goddamn business

So he found out

But all he knew was what others suspected was true

The look in his wife's eyes should have told him that months ago

But even if he wasn't a smart man, he didn't have to be so dumb

Mr. Legendre wasn't the type to tear things up though

He was as meek as a newborn babe suckling its mother's tit

Philomene had him wrapped around her finger twice

And when he showed any sign of raising up she showed him exactly which finger it was

-- The middle one --

Madame Marie had seen many grown men cry in her day over a woman

Then after she finished reading they'd fix their face real good before they left

No man wanted their neighbors, friends or even family to know how they really felt

Sometimes they cried harder than the women when they lost love

But they weren't as quick as the ladies to ask for the love to be fixed

When they did though -- and it did happen -- that man had to be drowning

He had to be soaked through to the bone and only asked because he couldn't live without her

Women did it even if she didn't know a man that well

Most of the time they didn't really love him, they just didn't want him to be with anybody else

You see, women fall in love faster

But men, they fall in love deeper -- that's why God made them slow to care

He protected them from suffering too much pain

That's why they think most of the time with that thing down there

Madame Marie wiped her granddaughter's mouth

It was shaped just like her mother's and her first husband's

As she watched Mr. Legendre put his face in his hands again and again

She hoped her grandbaby wouldn't be as cruel to her man as her mother was to him

Madame Marie tried to calm him down and asked him not to fret

She didn't tell him the trouble would be over soon with the intercession of the Saints.

6

I met Girard Andre at a bookstore

We were both browsing when the young man accidently bumped into me

The result of the collision was the young man's immediate recognition of my face

He remembered that I was the man that had been slandered again in the local paper

I prepared myself for a confrontation because he was obviously high up on the social ladder

He wore the finest of everything and had impeccable speech and manners

Though his accent was thicker than most, I complemented him on how well he spoke French

I learned that nothing pleases the coloreds of Creoledom more than hearing that statement from anyone

Especially if that someone has been to Paris

Monsieur Andre said he would be honored if I dined with him so that he may hear my side of the story

I warned him before accepting that I would make no attempt to censor any opinions that might offend him

For my speech was not a collar to be adjusted or starched

The man agreed and he prattled on about the weather and rising prices as we walked to the small café

I simply smiled, nodded and listened. Small talk? I never know what to say!

At the first place we tried, he wouldn't be able to sit

He had forgotten the license that stated he was free and rich

The second place weren't so friendly to coloreds whether they had a pass or not

Thirst. Frustration. Thirst. Frustration.

Two dry throats required libation and four aching legs desired a seat

So, Paschal asked the young man if he would like to come to his room for a drink

Once the brandy had been poured and rudimentary reviews of each other's lives were complete -- Girard wasted no time

He asked if it was true what the good people said,

That I was a whore mongering, heathen firebrand that roamed the streets at night

I was never so happy to say "emphatically yes" so much in my entire life!

Girard looked stunned before he laughed

He laughed like it was the first time he was ever allowed -- the picture of society he was

But as I shared my thoughts about life and living

I saw the man become less afraid -- to admit what he always knew

Girard at heart, is a libertine.

7

After Bella's client left she washed up and laid back down

She tried not to think about how she felt being with other men now

Paschal was the only man she wanted -- he was the only man she would ever want

She thought about how strange and wonderful it felt to be comfortably vulnerable and in love at the same time

But for her an independent woman love is impractical

A woman in her profession couldn't afford to feel

You see, when you sell pleasure -- be it cake, wine or pussy -- you have to be light

The customer can go anywhere to indulge their vice

That's why you must smile real wide, ask how they're doing and tell them you missed them if you haven't seen them in awhile

And once they buy whatever pleasure you're selling -- especially the one between your legs

You must never, ever forget to say -- please come again

Now that's all messed up because Bella is weighed down by thoughts of that one special guy

No client wants to hump on a woman with knees reluctant to part or honey water in her eyes

That's what one of her regulars said just a moment ago

Is that what her 7:00 o'clock will say to her too?

Are her days as a courtesan really through?

Bella inhaled and exhaled deeply -- what is she going to do?

I mean, she owned her own home and had plenty of money but Paschal wasn't the type to let her carry the weight

No, that man was as proud as proud can be -- and had no pimp in him

Bella asked an older woman she trusted how to go about a plan

"So, what do you do when you have more than a man, that's really a man?"

The woman laughed, shook her head then said "All you'll end up with is half man and half a whimpering pup,"

"If you want him to stay as gay as the day you met, then you'll have to live by his means and give it all up."

8

There were only fifteen slaves left at Clavijo plantation

The rest escaped North during all the commotion last year or ran off to join the Yankee soldiers

Thankfully, none of the house niggers caught *drapetomania because without them there wouldn't be enough servants to pull off a successful ball

Three of them did show signs of the disease but the overseer promptly provided them with effective remedies for weeks

Sadie had completely taken over the operations of the house because she said it needed a woman's touch

Though born and raised in Louisiana, she adapted quickly to Lowcountry ways

Now she insisted that the ceiling of the porch and the shutters be painted what they called "haint blue"

James didn't mind his sisters' aesthetic intrusions even though he found them to be frivolous and expensive --- but it made her happy

As Sadie sang and barked orders in the corridors, James sat in his study reviewing the guest list

One name had been added and crossed out several times

Paschal Beverly Randolph.

The most respected families of colored Creole society would be there

The Delilles, Galvez, Metoyers, Souliés, DuBuclets and so many others!

So the question was whether to stay true to self or remain faithful to norms

James wanted Dr. Randolph there

He was eccentric, acerbic and a personal friend of Abe Lincoln's -- But he also spoke French and was a good man

Though it would cause some talk, Sadie insisted that he be invited -- with a stern whip of her fan

"If he was good enough to be received by Napoleon le troisième than its fine."

James re-wrote Dr. Randolph's name and chuckled to himself

If he can dance well to Gottschalk they'll give him a chance!

*Drapetomania was a mental illness that, physician Samuel A. Cartwright hypothesized was the reason enslaved Blacks ran away.

9

Philomene tied her tignon and walked to Claiborne Avenue

Dawn was present but not yet perceptible to the eyes

But you could feel its vibration and hear a chorus of bird songs

She was on her way to St. Louis Cemetery to gather bits of limestone

The grave of a very brave soldier was there

Certainly by now the rock had absorbed some of his courage

That's why Doctor John told her to make some *Callioux brew

She had to get over her obsession with Dr. Randolph

She had to free herself from fantasies so deliciously sweet she dare not taste them

For if she did then generations to come would fall apart

Yes, she had to be free from her love

Free from the desire to live for one lifetime alone

Free from the temptation to destroy what her parents had built and create angry ghosts

So she walked on bathed in indigo twilight -- no one else would hear her solemn drudge

She wondered if she should smile as every step forward crushed so many of her dreams

After all, she was doing the right thing

Or was it best to still all emotions until the future came?

When she could cheer those few toddling steps towards another life once made

Yes, that's exactly what she would do!

She would become one of millions -- polishing bronzed baby shoes

Philomene finally arrived at her destination

Then she crossed herself three times before sneaking into the land of the dead -- through the secret way

So many souls clamored for her attention

They did that to anybody living that they knew could see

No one wanted to hurt her, they just wanted her to deliver messages to their people

Whoever they may be

When she finally found the resting place of Cailloux, Philomene stood at attention real straight and proud

She saluted the fallen soldier interred beneath her feet and the one within

Then laid down her shroud

When she gets home she will bathe and continue to be a dutiful mother and wife

The sorrowful song would then be over -- she would open a new umbrella to celebrate her life

*Andre Cailloux (1825 – 1863) was one of the first black officers in the Union Army to be killed in combat during the American Civil War.

10

Madame Marie waved goodbye to the last client she would ever see

Philomene and Emile would be together forever -- now she was through with Voodoo -- She kept her promise to thee!

Madame finally realized in the last few days

She had helped too many people to bash her past or grieve, her power was still a juicy orange -- that she just no longer wanted to squeeze.

PART TWO

"No one ever heard from his lips any indication from which it might be surmised that he shared in that superciliousness with which modern philosophers and thinkers frequently look upon other sciences and branches of knowledge. On the contrary, he took the deepest interest in human society, and all the branches that treat of men and social beings. He never fell into the grievous error of considering matter, space, force and time of higher importance than mind, society, right and goodness."

- Contemporary of P.B. Randolph

Chapter Five

"I am not P.B. Randolph; I am the voice of God,
crying, "Hold! Hold! to the nation in its mad career!
The lips of the struggling millions disfranchised
demanding justice in the name of Truth--a Peter the
Hermit, preaching a new crusade against Wrong, --the
Genius of progress appealing for schools; a pleader
for the people; a toiler for the millions yet unborn;
mechanic for the redemption of the world."

– P.B. RANDOLPH

PLEASURE BALL

In Honor of Mrs. Sadie Perchaud Greene

"While we live, let us Dance"

M Paschal Beverly Randolph

Is Requested To Attend the Ball,

At Clavijo Plantation, on Friday,

7 of October current at 8 o'clock P.M.

1

I am a mile away from Clavijo

One of many in a peacock caravan to Hollings' ball

Under normal circumstances I would have declined such an invitation

It is not a dislike of music and dance that invokes such disdain

It is the prodding for information that if asked directly, would be freely given

It is the obvious invocation of desire that must be denied or else be deemed impolite

It is the assumption that everyone present is happily stuck to the various webs that have been spun

But alas, I must go because Hollings had the courage to invite me

To refuse would have been cowardly and therefore unforgiveable

So

Here I am, in coat and tails -- a fitting outfit to wear as I enter the creole fire

But I wonder...

Which brown, gray or hazel eyes will attempt to incinerate me first?

Which belle will say they wish to slap me to their neighbor but later thrust forth their décolleté?

Which gentleman will have too much wine and request a good old fashioned duel?

None of that matters

For I am made of tempered glass -- I shall not melt or explode

But if perchance tonight I exist in a less fortified space, I am the most powerful phoenix I know

I would be lying if I didn't admit to having some curiosity about who and what will be awaiting me at this place

Along the way, I saw a beautiful woman and her chaperone -- they stopped along the side of the road

She wore a dress the color of the faintest rose

I smiled and she immediately gave hers in return

Then she leaned forward to retrieve a tear drop pearl that fell from the lobe of her left ear

A lady losing an earring was a common sight sure but for me it was nothing less than cataclysmic

All because a tiny lavender feather clung to her bosom

It took my breath away

But even more beautiful was the expression of horror on her face by the idea, that perhaps, I had seen more

When she realized I had been charmed by such a slight detail

She smiled again and turned her face

By the time her chaperone noticed something happened it was far too late

A highly erotic encounter had already taken place

In certain circles in Paris or New York upstate such occurrences were unnecessary because there was no chase

Group love sessions were as common as the innumerable theses that condemn sex outside of the marital bed

Attendees often being those that authored the treatises or their wives and daughters panting for relief

In the South, a man had to practically hypnotize a woman before she allowed her clitoris to be licked!

Free philosophies were almost unheard of here and if they were they would not be shared with free, willing women

Only in an uncivilized world did elegant rapists and love starved ladies make sense.

2

Bella wept as she clutched the invitation to the Clavijo ball to her chest

She could afford the same dresses and jewels as any other woman there but she couldn't go because she made the money on her own

On her back or on her knees

But it wasn't fair! Most of those honery bitches' men paid to have her that way!

So how come she had to stay home and their husbands could go?

Bella threw a boot at Paschal before he left

He thought speaking softly and patting her thigh was enough to soothe her wounded pride

What was the point in having the best of everything if no one wanted you around?

If you couldn't attend parties that didn't end with dead or drunken bodies strewn all over the ground?

No, ho life was no life at all

But neither was being a wife

She heard all about that sad state of affairs from her clients -- with all that whining, longing and strife

So what was the best way for a woman to live if she could live it true and full?

With no one to interrupt or correct her sentence before it was even through?

Paschal went on and on about freedom all the time because he didn't have the burdens that made women have to stay

Right where they are

In a somewhere, nowhere kinda place

Bella took a swig of liquor and winced

Then she went over to the drawer and looked at the broken tafo

Ohhh how she wished she could wrap it around one of those good belle's throats!

They would look at him with eyes she never had tonight

Eyes that never saw their mother dragged away in chains

Eyes that never saw a plate full of food being served while their stomach ached

Eyes that never considered how often other people not like them cried

Yes it was true, the only pupils they respect carried books in their arms

Never the ones in the eyes

Bella wondered if Paschal would find a new lover that he could whisper bigger words to

Someone that could really understand his mind instead of just pretending like she always had to do

More liquor

Wince

Liquor

Wince

Would she be the type that apologized a thousand times just because she sneezed?

Would she know the proper way to hold a fan, stand and sit?

She would probably know how to speak proper English, French and wit

Those are languages she never had the opportunity to master

Her story didn't include the unnecessary to make it fuller

No, it required the will to survive and the effrontery to expect even more than that

Her story didn't include imagining artificial paradises with Baudelaire or saluting the poesy of Timrod

No, it required the summoning of the devil's strength

Or maybe it was God's?

If Paschal wants a lamb as blemish free as a baby's soul, then let the saints sing tonight

Let them sing a song of victory as loud and proud as Clavijo himself

All is fair in love and war

Someone a long time ago said they're both the same

If she gets him I hope they both rot! God save St. James!

3

The floor manager looked frazzled as were the cloak room maids

Since when did everyone invited show up to a ball?

God save you! You'll need the patience of a saint tonight," a guest said to James

The promenade buzzed with the chatter of busy bees

While the orchestra played what everyone wanted to hear

The beauties and interesting ladies already had their dance cards filled with names

While those with less charms clung to their mother's arms, as the host kindly asked the other fellows that they be engaged

It had been such a long time since Hollings had entertained

But he did it for his sweet, sweet Sadie

His sister was made for glittering nights that even the moon remembered

When all that mattered in the world was the proper step to the right beat

When a ruffle at the edge of her dress transcended the world or caged her within it

Nights just like this

Tonight his sister wasn't the worried widow humming mournful songs on the porch when she thought no one was listening

Not even the ghost of Richard Greene could ruin an evening of spirits

That she drank -- heavily

There was no time for anyone to mourn the dead as the world itself gasped for breath

No time to think about what could have, would have or should have been

No time to shovel sarcastic or angry opinions on others regrets

Or to try to create them if they weren't already there

There was an astounding lack of interest in what tomorrow would bring

Whether it was to be a shower of cannonballs raining down upon them fired by Sherman -- or Lee

If the war taught them anything was that they knew not what really went on in Washington or Virginia anyway

The fingers of blame pointed in so many compass directions

Now all that mattered was today

This champagne fluted evening

This truffle filled dream

This evening that sweetens the tongue with chocolate meringue biscuits and cheese ice cream

Hollings laughed, really laughed with everyone for the first time in his life

Sadie noticed and so did all the rest

The band played but now they grooved

They played a little too uh...

Not the way they were supposed to

When did Renard loosen his cravat like that? What happened to prim proper Angelique?

When did the drums start playing and the hips start swaying?

When did this become a jamboree?

The realizations were too immense

The stark truth of it all was too intense to be believed

Confetti rain down! Confetti set us all free!

Roll all over the ground Mrs. Brown from the right side of town

We're all experts at being able to un-see!

The song is almost over -- wipe your brow and give your knee one more slap

The next tune is about to begin there ain't no time to clap!

Then

The trumpet sounded for the next dance to begin

And that's when Dr. Randolph walked in.

4

Girard Andre smirked when he saw his teacher stroll through the door

Paschal nodded cordially at everyone and looked amused as prim Mrs. Brown scrambled up from the floor

The servants standing behind him looked around in shock at the gens de couleur libres acting *really* colored

Then hastily exited before the high yellas remembered what they had to forget

The floor manager announced the doctor as if he was nervous about what to expect

Hollings made his way to the front of the room and escorted the man in

To reintroduce the people that feared, loved and hated him

If Dr. Randolph was nervous he showed nothing at all

He shook and kissed hands, bowing ever so gracefully

The women were smitten and the men were impressed -- reluctantly

His popularity made the bloodhounds roll their eyes and suck their teeth

In the shadows, of course, where they always wanted to be

Then he saw Sadie talking to the woman he saw on the road, the one with the Rose colored dress

And got that look on his face

Girard steered him away and gestured for the floor manager to strike up the music again

Dr. Randolph danced so well!

It was a sight to see, the way he strutted and spun those ladies around the floor

Many were surprised because he seemed to prefer the older ones first

Which only made the younger women want him even more

But Girard knew that's not why he did it -- the unexpected to him was just fun

"No" the doctor said, I chose them because their bodies have more to say,

They have more pickle on the bun lad," -- or so he claimed

But the woman in the rose colored dress watched him like she knew him

Like she wanted to know him -- in that special kind of way

Girard gasped when he saw other women looking at him desiring too

"I don't know how you do it man, it must be that Voodoo!"

Dr. Randolph asked the young man in a serious tone to step outside

The owls hooted softly and the crickets were loud

He denied that his power came from Voodoo but from the white fire inside

"What's that?" Girard asked.

"The fluid of bliss, learn to re-route your joy son."

Electricity and Lightning is actually love?

"If a man cannot control himself in the bedroom, how could he ever control anything outside of it without brute force?"

Girard watched as his teacher drew diagrams with his fingers in space

And somehow the cosmos didn't seem so meaningless anymore

But he was still perplexed

"Bon homme you confuse me!" Girard said.

Dr. Randolph told him to focus or his lessons would be of no use

"The white fire huh," Girard chuckled to himself, "I'm seventeen! I've got plenty of juice!"

5

Sadie frowned when she saw Dr. Randolph happily chatting in the corner with Armand Lanusse

They were both troublemaking writers so she guessed it only made sense

But for a staunch confederate, her brother sure had a lot of abolitionist friends!

"Oh who cares," she thought -- the New Yorker was awful cute and he liked her dress

Sadie's mind still spun -- A Yankee in her father's home -- Oh Lord what was this world coming to!

She turned to a woman that knew her since she was young, "If daddy could get up out of that tomb Junior would be spitting nothing but teeth and excuses."

The gray haired woman 'hmphed' in agreement and kept it moving

The thought made Sadie laugh to herself but she had to admit she liked the controversy

Look at those old hens flapping their jaws…

She reckoned all artists were the same way because inside they were mostly just tired and bored

Besides, whatever repercussions come from all this eccentricity wasn't her problem

New Orleans wasn't really home anymore

Sadie spoke English all the time in Charleston and well…Catholicism

Just didn't feel as right as it did before

But it was great to see familiar faces and hear familiar sounds

It was almost three in the morning and the ball was still going strong

And that Dr. Randolph

My how the ladies hung on that man's every word!

Fanning and giggling their way all the way through

Sadie listened to the stories too

Only three walked away because the man said shocking things

But at least he did it in a side-door way and you had to be quick to get it

It was a curious thing because her brother described him almost as half dead

And then that comment he made to Vivian Andre about how the world would be different if people told the truth

Girard's aunt didn't like it at all and calmly said "Les coqs ne font pas surgir le soleil."

"Ah, Dr. Randolph said, Indeed roosters don't make the sun come up!"

Sadie was happy to see him put in his place but at the same time she didn't – it was something about him…

It must have been the Louisiana heat that was getting to her

There was no salt in the air like there was in Charleston

She was used to those refreshing breezes provided by the sea

Sadie looked at Dr. Randolph again -- yes that's what it was -- the Creole fire

That's what it had to be.

Chapter Six

"The ejective moment, therefore, is the most divine and tremendously important one in the human career as an independent entity; for not only may we launch Genius, Power, Beauty, Deformity, Crime, Idiocy, Shame or Glory on the world's great sea of Life, in the person of the children we may then produce, but we may plunge our own souls neck-deep in Hell's horrid slime, or else mount the Azure as coequal associate Gods; for then the mystic Soul swings wide its Golden gates, opens its portals to the whole vast Universe and through them come trooping either Angels of Light or the Grizzly Presence from the dark corners of the Spaces. Therefore, human copulation is either ascentive and ennobling, or descensive and degrading…"

– P.B. RANDOLPH

You are cordially invited to an

AFTERNOON TEA

Tuesday, The Twenty-Fifth of October, at One O'Clock

Clavijo Plantation

Hostess: Mrs. Sadie Perchaud Greene

1

Here I sit for the second time in Hollings' parlour

It is a grand space decorated in the typical New Orleanian way

All of the antique furnishings are opulently gilded and tufted

Velvet upholstered Begere chairs and colored crystals dangle from chandeliers

An elaborate ceiling medallion staring from above like the eye of Horus

Portraits of their relatives revolve about the space

Their skins all white, tan and beige --- zodiacal glyphs for their guests to admire their sang-mêlé

Every bit of it an exotic chaos I can understand

Sadie and her brother sat differently in this room than in any other

Sadies' posture was more erect while James's became more relaxed

I can't help but wonder which pair of painted eyes caused that?

James' slave, a striking *griffe they called "Oxhorn" then entered the room

"Mr. Valmour has arrived Massa."

I couldn't look at him

Sadie felt my discomfort -- James just knew it was there

And didn't care

"There he is, finally, Dr. Randolph this is John Valmour," said Sadie.

The conversation proceeded like spring rain

In the beginning, delicate and light then torrential the next minute

Monseiur Valmour was one of the founding members of Cercle Harmonique

And a virulent -- anti Catholique

The spiritualist embraced me awkwardly as he claimed to be my biggest fan

Before excitedly explaining to our jaw dropped hosts, my theory of Pre-Adamite man

Sadie sipped her tea and periodically looked at me

With wise eyes I hadn't noticed before today and a cordial smile plastered upon her face

It was so fake

But so necessary to survive the life fate forced her to live

Or requested? Something tells me that if she could choose...

Her reality, for the most part, would be exactly the same

I don't know whether to praise this fact or mourn it

My confusion is perpetual yet I see everything so clear

She is a mantua maker -- a fashioner of exquisite cloaks

That is what she does and apparently, who she is as well

James noticed me staring at his sister as Valmour continued to speak

Then he realized her complicity

Sadie tilts her head and takes tiny sips -- with extra pursed lips

Big brother watches as his little sister strokes her cup with her little finger

And interrupts her pantomime of what it could be like with her alone…

After dark.

*A Griffe was the offspring of a mulatto and a Black person.

2

"Let's run away together."

Bella closed her eyes

She had heard those words a thousand times – but only from parched, trembling or bleeding lips

Pietro saw her buying flowers and begged to be let back in

It felt good to be with him again

Not only because he was a good lover and kind of a friend

But because he was clear about how he felt about her

He didn't drift away when she spoke too long -- to some distant place

Some place that he couldn't describe but say he couldn't live without visiting

Every. Single. Day.

A location so remote that once reached

That only pieces of you fell back to the Earth

Bella ran her fingers through Pietro's hair as he kissed her breasts

He was trying to get her started again

The money was on the table and it was twice or three times more than he usually paid

She felt sorry for him

Poor Pietro, the fool that didn't care that he was

Bella patted his head for him to stop

She was done

"Forget him Bella, no one will ever love you like I do,"

Bella closed her eyes

She never heard those words before

And if they could magically appear in a jewelry shop window

Oh, how they would sparkle and shine!

Then he produced a circle of gold he hid underneath the pillow

A proposal in a world of black and white might as well be a ring of fire

And not the kind where people clap when you survive

But one that wants to watch you burn for even trying

Pietro wanted to take on a world that didn't want to be taken on

He wanted to take a walk on the dark side

Just because it felt right

Bella smiled at Pietro and held up the circle of gold in the sunlight

"Let's leave America where it's possible for us to marry legally."

Her arm flopped back down on the bed

Leave America?

Chains. Prejudice. Limitations. Broken Promises. Rape. Assault. Murder

Repeat

And Repeat

And Repeat

Leave America?

But there was still hope and her ancestors were still in *this* soil

As was a love that burns brighter than Pietro's desire

A love that is strong enough to eventually open Paschal's eyes

And convince his mouth

To form the same words emitted by a man she didn't really want

A love that was so true it would force him to make the right choice

Bella closed her eyes again

To imagine the proposal being asked with the right voice.

3

Even though Sadie had been married four years before her husband died

James didn't see her that way -- until today

I mean, he knew theoretically that she was no longer a virgin

But damn, did she have to be that much not like one?

James didn't like the way she shimmied her shoulders as she removed her shawl

He didn't like the way she nodded her head when Dr. Randolph spoke

And he didn't like the way she asked if he wanted more cream in his tea

Paschal was a man so of course he liked the attention

Though James couldn't tell if he really wanted to bed her or not

He knew the doctor well enough to know there was often more to his gaze than what was apparent

But sometimes there wasn't

Paschal had been with many women -- all over the world too

Despite all that coquette nonsense

Sadie was too innocent -- and that white fire technique -- she wouldn't know what to do!

"How did you and Mr. Valmour meet?" asked Dr. Randolph.

"We have a mutual friend named *Henri Rey. He's an old friend from my Native Guard days." said James.

The men got into a heated discussion about the outcome of the war and other things

Then Sadie got uptight and blurted out "I helped free fourteen of my slaves."

The men listened as she spoke of her support of Negroes colonizing Liberia

That's where she arranged for Goober to return to

And transported Cicero, Jenny and Wade

She said she helped the others purchase their freedom by hiring them out

And then let them keep their pay

James eyes widened as his little sister spoke

As did the other two men

They all thought Sadie was just another southern belle!

James wanted to cry

Where had his sweet, sweet Sadie gone?

The Sadie that didn't care if those pickaninnies sewed until dawn?

Dr. Randolph praised the compassion of Mrs. Greene

Then Valmour blurted out, "If the spirit world could be replicated on this plane than we'd all be free!"

James didn't like to admit it but he always liked spirit talk and spirit people

But that talk should stay somewhere out there -- don't mess with nobody's money

Enough was enough!

Sadie passed out more finger sandwiches

Then some fancy lemon bars

Then more tea and conversation about ideal new worlds appearing after the war was over

The discussion had gone way too far.

---

*Henri Rey (d. 1876), was one of the founding members of the Cercle Harmonique, a group of predominantly men of African descent that heavily practiced Spiritualism in New Orleans.

4

"If I tell you a secret you promise not to tell anyone?" Girard asked his best friend.

Jomy Brown shook his head yes and leaned forward to listen

Girard told him about his forbidden teacher and the white fire thing

As Jomy listened to the whole story quietly

Then Girard talked about the men that existed before Adam and the advanced Negroes of the future that were sure to come

Then about blending with spiritual consciousness -- that's when Jomy was done

He asked his friend why he conversed regularly with a mad man that didn't mean him well

A man with a foul reputation, lewd thoughts and obviously destined for hell

Girard tried to keep Jomy from walking away from him

He hadn't finished telling him about all the interesting things he was learning

And why it wasn't foolish

But Jomy was as straight laced as they come

In fact, if Jomy Brown had created the ocean there wouldn't be any waves

There was more excitement in a dying man's sigh than Jomy Brown's imagination

He just liked things to be right where he found them

He wanted everyone and everything to stop not being the same

Jomy was the most affected by the war out of all of his peers

Girard knew that

But he thought he could give good reasons to eliminate fears

If enough people heard how life *could* be they'd change, wouldn't they?

At least, that's what Girard believed

Maybe people all over the world will be connected one day he thought

Then they would communicate, Yeah that'd be great...

Girard strolled back home from Jomy's house feeling excited for the humanity to come

He'd be dead by then but in a hundred years there would be peace

And everybody living as one

But before that first things first

Girard couldn't wait to celebrate the Union's victory!

It was about time that Creoles and Negroes united strong

For if the confederates won the divisions among non-whites would only prolong

His mother told him not to ever think of taking some newly freed Negro beast as a bride

The consequences she said would be in two generations

Nappy hair, poverty, no culture or pride

Girard wiped the tears from his cheeks when he recalled that speech

He never felt different than his great grandmother's people a day in his life

Jomy did though

He agreed with all that stuff just like everyone else

Girard was different in so many ways since the day he breathed his first breath

His father hit him to make him stop talking to trees and they had to force feed him animal flesh

He read controversial books and gave serious thought to what others said never could be

Then when he met P.B. Randolph, he delved even further into the realm of possibilities.

5

Sadie waved as Valmour and Dr. Randolph left Clavijo

Her brother thought they would leave the best of friends but it wasn't to be

According to him, Valmour found Dr. Randolph dull in person and Dr. Randolph found Valmour an affable but redundant personage he's met too many times

Sadie found Dr. Randolph's assessment shocking since she never met anyone like either of them and she found Valmour's perspective partially true

She agreed that Dr. Randolph could be way more fun

Unlike Valmour she saw how charming he could be at the ball

Sadie kissed her brother and retreated to her room

She said she wanted to take a nap but she retired to help him

The poor man still looked as jealous and angry as the brothers of Joseph

But it wasn't her fault he still thought of her as a girl

That was a long time ago

Before the death of her husband and the murder of her child

Before she barely survived the attempt to take her own life

No one knew about that but a trusted slave that worked in the house

It was a beautiful day to die too

The weather was real nice -- not a cloud in the sky

Except a small one far off in the distance shaped like a slaughtered calf

She had eaten shrimp and grits that day

Her favorite meal

And Sadie made Wade play her favorite song on the fiddle

But then she made him stop because she didn't deserve to feel good

She didn't deserve to smile

Sadie curled up on the bed and cried because she was a liar

She cried because the memories of the past, conflicted with the reality she manufactured for others to remember

There was no sweet Sadie

Just a clever weaver of broken threads

Just an idea of what once was

Sadie buried her face in a pillow so she could scream

The baby was murdered

And she said it was alright.

Chapter Seven

"All there is in us worth Immortalizing, worth
preserving and presenting to the Infinite is our love
nature and our Will power; which must begin at home
[as does charity], if at all. By virtue of our Will we
control ourselves, and when we are perfect masters of
ourselves—our passions, thoughts, desires, etc., we
will be Masters of God's universe of lesser Nature.
How many are there who can truly say in the face of
adverse storms, and feel what they say: Let the winds
blow high or low, the thunders of evil roll, and the
lightning's glare, I am above it all. Do your worst— I
was here first!"

– P.B. RANDOLPH

1

I received a letter that I was to be accepted back at the Negro School

This dog has, once again, been given a tasty treat for kissing the buttocks of the colored Creole elite

But I had to do it because my ambitions are long and my money is short -- not nearly enough to last

Perhaps one day I will be able to save enough to escape soul rape -- I hate the taste of ass!

If they were partial to serious self-reflection, they would realize they are not so different than the Blacks they despise

If they could but sojourn to the inner east and open their third eyes

Yes, their naiveté and willingness to break bread so soon after insult was just as evident as Africa's stupid men

Their noble blood is a most welcome cosmetic alteration, but if pure, would not have given me another chance

For if it was, I would be unable to lullaby them as quickly -- with a well-coordinated speech, song and dance

I can't stop re-reading the letter because it makes me laugh

At them

At that stupid ball

At myself…

I miss New York.

No matter how near or far I travel from her, that is the thought my heart eventually thinks

It's the last place I saw my mother laugh

It's the host of childhood ghosts

The white cat that stalks my path appeared again this evening and curled up on my writing desk for a nap

I pet my spy, familiar and friend often and occasionally let it sleep in my lap

I'm tired of desiring a perfect way to exist in the world and I'm tired of trying to find my proper place

The truth has always been I am neither Black, White, Indian or any other race

Paschal Beverly is simply a husk masking an extra-terrestrial within

A brilliant, sulking alien experimenting with a human skin

The smoke from the hashish billows out of the window like a cloud

I wonder where the impressions of my thoughts will go

They must travel -- because they are alive like me and the people that walk along the French Quarter below

"The mind is the lab of real alchemists," said General Hitchcock to me in Germany.

As I stood amidst a circle of my elder brothers of degree

It was there I met men that sat upon Taunus' peaks and took notes von der Höhe -- to distill purer or as they translated in English -- "from the height"

Now eight years later, I'm in another city Décoré avec lillies questioning my role as anyone's "knight"

And if the steed upon which I ride is true

My conscience begs me to ask myself "Which kind of knight are you?"

Is it the lustful man with the erect baton, the hardworking pessimist with the coin or the hypersensitive daydreamer carrying only big ideas that amount to nothing in his cup?

Or

Is it the tactless, intolerant pedantic with words abrupt?

I know now I must leave Louisiana

I should leave before both the good and bad boy acts wear thin

I must depart before the men forced to pledge allegiance explode when the union wins.

2

Bella hated when people licked their fingers before they turned a page

Paschal did that when he read one of his high hattin books

So she knocked it out of his hand, folded her arms and gave him a scornful look

He nodded his head as if he deserved what she did or like he understood

She hated when people did that too

"Okay Bella, I think I know what's wrong but tell me what did I do?"

Bella knocked everything off of his desk

"Looka here and see what I do to your fuck potions also!" she shouted.

Then she sent a few bottles crashing to the floor

Bella was a whirlwind in that room

A whirlwind of rage, beauty and something that resembled confidence to those equally less self-assured

Paschal watched calmly as his lover destroyed his property and self-respect

He had known for a long time she was in love with him and wanted to be his only one

He also knew that despite his great affection for her -- it could never be done

As the feathers from his mutilated pillows drifted softly down from the ceiling to the floor

The white cat observed and began to play

After exhaustion collapsed Bella into a sobbing heap upon the bed --

Paschal removed his shirt

Then he dipped his finger into the spilled ink and drew an 'X' across his chest

It took Bella a few moments to realize he was just standing there

Watching her

With no expression

She destroyed most of his stuff and still

No reaction.

Her finger pointed at the 'X', "Why did you do that?"

She was afraid he had finally snapped

Then he reached into the drawer and pulled out a revolver

Bella never even knew it was there!

Because she would have shot him if she had

"This is what you want isn't?" he asked.

Paschal then kissed the barrel and tried to place it in her hands

Bella grabbed the gun and then kicked him so hard he stumbled back

It took Bella a few seconds to realize he was still just standing there

Watching her

With no expression

She kicked him and now she was pointing a gun at him and still

No reaction.

She dropped the gun and kicked it across the room

It hit the screen behind him and he looked

"I'm through with you Paschal. You should have never told me you loved me when you knew you couldn't choose."

Dr. Randolph waved his hand at her and laughed then he picked up a cigarette and lit it

Bella wanted to crawl between his legs, grab the gun and blow his head off!

"Oh, you think this is funny?"

Paschal blew out a stream of smoke "Of course not, honey,"

Men.

They want you to love them but as soon as you do

It ain't long before they think it's funny or tiresome

Women.

They want you to love them but as soon as you do

They want you frozen in amber, owned or possessed

Bella wept as all the reasons why they couldn't be together rained down around her

They landed on the floor too -- only much harder than the feathers

Maybe he didn't understand her

Or maybe he didn't believe a word she said

Bella had to make it clear that she would be forever distant if he didn't commit

That any feelings she had for him would be left for dead

Then she showed him the ring she carried against her bosom

The one she hadn't had the strength to fully accept quite yet

Dr. Randolph examined the golden circle Bella held out to him in her quivering hand

Surely he would immediately cry out and concede defeat if he knew she would marry another man!

It took Bella a few seconds to realize he just stood there

Watching her

With no expression

She showed him her engagement ring and told him she would leave America -- but still

No reaction.

3

Hollings flipped a few coins in Philomene's basket before he sat down to be read

It had been a long time since he had seen his Voodoo friend

She made them coffee and sat down at the table

He could tell she had a slight attitude like she always did whenever her better clients hosted a ball

Philomene was never invited

She couldn't be

People like her were reserved for life's curb

To separate the road from the roadside and provide structural support to the main way -- from the edge

Hollings was uncomfortable as she cast a handful of items onto a piece of cloth

They fell in all kinds of directions but mostly on the left hand side

That's when Philomene leaned forward to analyze them and grunted

"Someone you know did a terrible thing James, something that they never want you to know. This person is from somewhere else but now they're real close."

Hollings got up from the table so Philomene wouldn't see so much emotion

"Do you know who it is?" asked the priestess.

James nodded and shook his head, "There's only one person it could be."

Hollings told her everything that happened at the ball and at afternoon tea

Philomene sprinkled holy water over her, James' head and the loon bone that exposed Sadie's hypocrisy

Sweet Sadie

His dear, sweet Sadie

Where had she gone?

What has she done?

Philomene said she couldn't see the crime because it had been cleverly hidden by…someone

James slammed his fist against the wall

He couldn't hold back the sobs that had been building up any longer

"The truth will come out if you confront her about it. Whatever it is has been a great burden and she'll tell you if you don't let her run."

Tears welled up in James' eyes but before he walked out of the door he asked, "Can you at least tell me what it's about?"

Philomene sucked her teeth "What else but some man she had no business messin with?"

"Thank you."

Then James walked out.

Goddamn this Louisiana Heat!

He tried to wave the rays away

He tried to block out the sun

Philomene wouldn't have mentioned the man if Sadie just pecked him on the cheek

But who could have seduced her

Then it hit him and his knees got weak

It was that scoundrel Dr. Randolph!

He had taken advantage of his little sister! That's why she was acting so strangely!

James felt a rage so hot it made him crack his knuckles as he walked

There was nowhere that whack Moses could go!

If he was home James was going to loosen up his jaw

He was going to give that man a beating like he never gave another

Except Lucie...

Then after he looked like the devil danced with him -- he'd choke the life right outta him

Yes, folks for miles around would talk about the condition of his body for years in tones hushed and grim.

4

Girard sat quietly with his head down as his father ranted and raved

All he kept repeating was "I'm disappointed in you son."

They were always disappointed about something

He wish he could get away from New Orleans, his parents and everyone he knew

It didn't matter that he was happy with the decisions he made, all they ever cared about were their stupid rules!

Girard wanted to live by his *own* rules and believe whatever *he* wanted to believe

He wanted to figure things out for himself and be free to make mistakes

Everyone talked about how sad being orphaned was but at least they didn't have to be constantly nagged and fussed over!

Girard's mother wasn't in the room while he was being scolded but he knew she was listening behind the door

She always did that

Then she would pretend to know nothing as she embroidered flowers, acting all innocent

Jomy should have never been trusted with his big secret or none of this would have never happened

Now he would have to stop visiting Dr. Randolph

He would have to stop learning

He would have to stop growing -- for the sake of the family

That made no sense to him

What is the purpose of life then? Surely, the point was not to isolate oneself from everyone that doesn't live and think exactly as we do

Or is it?

That's what all animals on Earth do though, didn't they?

Girard's father spoke passionately about the importance of preserving their ways for future generations

If the family became something else, if *he* did something else

Than their culture would be forgotten, *they* would all be forgotten, he said

And it would all be Girard's fault because it sure wasn't going to be his docile sister Berdine to break with tradition

Then it hit him

The reason his parents were so frightened was because they didn't want to be erased

In other words, it was the common man's way of trying to achieve immortality

That's what Dr. Randolph would probably say

When the doctor said 'common' he wasn't talking about money or breeding but the level of mind people had

Girard suddenly didn't resent his parents so much

He began to understand.

5

Sadie hesitated a moment before she knocked on Valmour's door

She frowned at all the tools and scrap metal strewn about

He was a blacksmith by day and communicated with spirits at night

The sound of that child taking its last breath kept haunting her

As did the twitching it did after that long needle had been removed from its skull

Carol told her that she shouldn't have watched Wade do it, that she should have made him take the baby out to the shed

Sadie didn't listen but she wished she had

She ignored Carol because she felt it was bad enough that the child had to die

At the very least, it could still be with its mother -- for a little while

Valmour suddenly opened the door and smiled

Sadie could see the other Cercle Harmonique members behind him inside

The room was already candlelit and dark

"Come in Mademoiselle," he said with a genteel bow

There were five other people there besides herself and Valmour

One was a woman they called "Sister Louise"

Sadie took a deep breath as she sat down to calm her nerves but all she did was taste steel

Valmour introduced her to the other spiritualists but no one seemed interested in being formally introduced

There were people that could see into in the great beyond

People that could see inside *you*

Sadie felt nude

"Now that we're all here let us close our eyes and pray," said Sister Louise

Sadie folded her hands and squinted her eyes tightly -- she was still very scared

Valmour's booming voice as he recited the invocation didn't help

Every time he said 'illuminate' felt like a crack of thunder in her soul

And every time he appealed to 'the eternal and infinitely good father' to guide them -- she wanted to run

She might have to, if there were somewhere to go -- a place with an address where one could seek refuge from guilt and shame

The man across from her began to twitch

The man on her left began to sweat

And Valmour just stared blankly ahead

The others were in various states of departure from this realm

It was clear no one was fully present in this world but her

It felt like the room was closing one minute and expanding the next

Then Sister Louise burst out laughing but everyone knew she wasn't there

They had a visitor

The sweaty man dashed over to a table behind them to retrieve a paper and pen

"So you came back home to find a way to get rid of me again?"

Sister Louise' eyes were still closed but the spirit made her smile wide

"Uh, good evening Sir or Ma'am, welcome. Don't be afraid alright, we're good people here,"

The spirit cackled and banged its fist on the table

Everyone looked at each other with shocked faces

Sadie began to fan herself because it was so hot -- and to hide her terror

"Please Sir or Ma'am, tell us who you are," asked the twitching man.

"Don't call me that! I never got the chance to become a Ma'am because of her,"

The spirit pointed at Sadie then began to weep and rub the top of her head

"Oh Lord have Mercy what is going on?" asked another guy at the end of the table

Everyone looked from Sadie to the angry spirit

"I don't know what kind of devilishment this is! I've made a terrible mistake coming here!" said Sadie.

She ran for the front door

"Don't you even *think* of walking out that door mama or I promise you...you won't make it home. Now sit down!"

Sadie did as she was told and began to sob. "Stop bothering me Julia! You *know* why you had to die!"

Chapter Eight

"I do not represent the three-fourths black; I stand here to-night as representative of the African. I do not come as a flatter of the black man; I want justice for him…Who are we, that are now nothing before the world? The best blood that runs in the veins of any people runs in ours. We claim our rights because we are men, fashioned by the hand of Almighty God…There are two questions that come up: the one is the question of social equality, the other, of political equality. All men, so far as humanity is concerned, are not equal for the reason that a man is better than another man. The only aristocracy of mind and morals; the best man stands the highest. His spirit of democracy is to fight for universal rights."

– P.B. RANDOLPH

1

Pietro gazed into Bella's eyes after the priest said "You may kiss the bride."

Bella puckered her lips but all Pietro could do was plant a forehead kiss -- and cry

The father was kind to marry them in a secret ceremony in the cathedral basement

It didn't matter though because no one would have celebrated their love anyway

Pietro was disowned by his family when they were told his plan

His father said if he would have known one of his children would sink so low, they would have never came to this land

And his mother in the meantime -- kept screaming and biting the side of her hand

"Why was she doing that?" Bella asked.

Pietro laughed. "What? The hand thing? Everyone does that where I'm from when they get really mad."

"Shit, you Italians are crazy! That's why it's better to move to France."

Pietro helped the new Mrs. Giordano onto the steamboat, to start a new life free of bigotry and prejudice in Paris

Bella wasn't sure if it was going to be everything people said it was but she had to see

So she sold her house and Pietro sold his business so they'd have plenty of money

As the boat left the port of Lake Pontchartrain

Bella couldn't help but look the other way

She mourned the life she could have had with her beloved Paschal

But she was happy about the life she saved.

2

James watched as Carol darted back and forth collecting Sadie's belongings

His sister decided abruptly that it was time to leave and wouldn't hear of remaining in New Orleans another day

"Get out." James said to the slave.

"Sir?" she asked quizzically before the look in his eyes told her she should obey

"Tell everyone in the house to go to! Me and Ms. Sadie are about to have it out!"

James pulled back the drapes to make sure that the Negroes followed his orders

Then he climbed the stairs -- slowly

Because he knew that whatever was revealed to him would change everything

He knocked firmly on Sadie's bedroom door

"Come in!" she said.

James did and stood there waiting

"Oh hello James, I thought you were Carol bringing more of my things,"

James watched his sister fluffing her curls at the cream vanity table their father gave her

"What's wrong? Why are you standing there blinking your eyes at me like a goat?"

"That's enough Sadie. I want to know."

Sadie smoothed out her eyebrows and rose to face her brother

"I don't know what you're talking about,"

James smacked her across the face but not as hard as he could have

"How dare you!"

Then Sadie smacked him back

The slaves were all outside watching and though they could see some of what was going on they couldn't hear a thing

"I didn't do anything wrong! I don't care what anybody said!"

But James was breathing mighty heavily and his nostrils flared

"Don't lie to me you little whore, I know you did something with that man!"

Sadie looked up at her brother with the widest eyes he had ever seen

James balled up his fist and shook it in front of her -- he didn't care that he was being mean

That's when Sadie burst into tears

"I was so lonely after Richard died. I took it harder than anyone could ever know. I thought I was going to die too from missing him so much. I didn't mean for a baby to come."

James lowered his fist, "What?"

It became clear that her secret had nothing to do with Dr. Randolph

Sadie walked over to her writing desk and sat with her back to her brother

"Who was the man Sadie?" James asked with a tight jaw

Sadie cried some more

"I told Cicero, that big black slave I had, to come see me that night."

James felt lightheaded and flopped down on her bed

Sadie swallowed hard and continued her tale of lust and betrayal

"I needed him James, I told you I needed somebody. Anybody to block out the pain. Honestly, I had never been with a Black before or since."

James felt sick to his stomach "And you got pregnant by *him*?"

Then he hung his head in shame and sorrow

"Yes, I hid it well though. You knew from before.. that I'm one of those women that carry small. So, I told Carol to tie my corset as tight as she could. I thought I could squeeze it out."

James lifted his head, "So where's the baby now?"

"Dead."

Sadie then turned around with a calm look on her face *"We needled it"

A whimper escaped James lips and then he cried

Sadie then rushed to his side and embraced him

She wiped the tears from his face and sighed

"I gave the child two weeks but it kept getting darker and darker. I had no choice but to say goodbye."

James shrugged her off and paced back and forth with his head in hands

"But Sadie you could have just sold it, how could you kill your own child?"

"Because unlike you dear brother I couldn't stand to see my child sold and hogtied!"

James rushed over and grabbed his sister by the shoulders

"You're nothing but a murderer. At least now, thanks to Lincoln, Lucie's niglets have a chance!"

Though every bone in Sadie's body were firm, James could tell that his words crushed her

James released Sadie and decided to leave her alone before either of them could say anymore

As James ran down the stairs enraged

He heard a bang

When he ran back up he prayed it wasn't what he thought it was

Then James flung open the door

And there was Sadie

No longer with a head on her shoulders, lying on the floor.

---

*Black infants were often killed by inserting a needle in their brain through the fontanel. Doctors and midwives used this technique to get rid of evidence that white women had been sexually involved with enslaved Black men.

3

I am packing my bags

I am returning to New York

Like the doomed philosopher Socrates, I have been accused of corrupting the youth

The offer to teach has been rescinded

The Brown and Andre families have slandered my name and by doing so, dashed any possibility of remaining in this city

So, once again

I am an outcast

Once again, man exchanges manna from heaven for molded bread

Here I am once more, associated with the devil

Here is the latest edition to add to humanity's already voluminous journal of absurdities regarding this issue

If there was a devil, he too would be my son because I'm God

As they are

But they're too stupid to know.

Farewell New Orleans!

Adieu my beautiful Vieux Carré -- How I loved you so.

EPILOGUE

Paschal Beverly Randolph (1825-1875) visited New Orleans between1863-1865 where he lectured on a variety of subjects and worked as a teacher. He planned to write about the Blacks of Louisiana but he died under mysterious circumstances before that happened.

Dr. Randolph never met or interacted in any way with any of the historically based characters mentioned in this book except for Napoleon III (1808-1873), General Ethan Hitchcock (1798-1870) and President Abraham Lincoln (1809-1865) whom he considered a very close friend.

The dates of birth/death of the historical personages included in this fictional account are as follows:

Marie LaVeau - (1801-1881), Vodou Priestess

Marie Philomene Glapion Legendre - (1836-1897), Vodou Priestess

John Valmour (aka John B. Averin) - (?-1869), Spiritualist

Jean "Dr. John" Montaigne - (1815 - 1885), Root worker/Hoodoo Man

"Sister Louise" - (d. 1868 or 1869), Spiritualist

Armand Lanusse - (1810 – 1868), Poet

Dear Reader,

Thank you for purchasing *Creole Fire*. If you enjoyed the book, please write a review on Amazon and spread the word on social media, it's the best way for independent authors and authors with small publishers to gain exposure. I also invite you to like the *Creole Fire* page on Facebook and Follow me on Instagram. If you'd like to send me a personal message and/or to be added to my contact list, please email me at: TayannahLee@gmail.com

Sincerely,
Tayannah

Made in the USA
San Bernardino, CA
17 May 2020

71783716R00100